Between Mom and Jo

Between Mom and Jo

by Julie Anne Peters

Megan Tingley Books

LITTLE, BROWN AND COMPANY

New York ❧ Boston ❧ London

Also by Julie Anne Peters:

Define "Normal"
Far from Xanadu
Keeping You a Secret
Luna

Little, Brown and Company

Time Warner Book Group
1271 Avenue of the Americas, New York, NY 10020
Visit our Web site at www.lb-teens.com

First Edition: May 2006

Library of Congress Cataloging-in-Publication Data
Peters, Julie Anne.
Between Mom and Jo / by Julie Anne Peters. — 1st ed.
p. cm.
Summary: Fourteen-year-old Nick has a three-legged dog named
Lucky 2, some pet fish, and two mothers, whose relationship
complicates his entire life as they face prejudice, work problems,
alcoholism, cancer, and finally separation.
ISBN 0-316-73906-5 (hardcover)
[1. Mothers and sons — Fiction. 2. Lesbians — Fiction.
3. Family problems — Fiction. 4. Prejudices — Fiction.] I. Title.
PZ7.P44158Bet 2006
[Fic]—dc22   2005022012

10 9 8 7 6 5 4 3 2 1

Q-FF
Printed in the United States of America

To Claudia Mills,

who greatly exceeds expectations in every department

Jo

I'm sitting on a cold metal slab, and there's blood all over my shirt. I've been screaming so long my throat's raw. Jo leaps out from behind the door and goes, "Ha!"

You know those sticks doctors gag you with when they're looking down your throat? Tongue depressors. Jo's slid two of them up under her top lip. In a goofy voice she says, "I'm Wally Walrus. Tusk. Tusk." One of the tongue depressors falls out. "Oops," Jo says. "Make that tusk." She bends over to retrieve the stick off the floor.

Through my blur of tears I see something on her butt. I hiccup and point.

"What?" Jo bolts upright. She reaches back. "Oh, hey. I wondered where that went." She peels a gummy worm off her jeans and slurps it into her mouth. I giggle a little.

Jo clutches her throat, staggering backward like she's

poisoned. She knocks a box of latex gloves off the counter and curses. I can't see her as she's picking up the box, but I hear blowing sounds. Cautiously I peer over the edge of the table.

Jo shoots up, and I yelp. She's filled a glove with air and twisted it at the wrist, and she's holding it in the middle of her head. She's bobbing and strutting around the room going, "Cock-a-doodle-doo. Cock-a-doodle" — reaching out a claw to grab me. She pecks at me. Her eyes are evil and she's going to get me. Just as I shriek, the doctor bursts in. He looks from Jo to me.

"Who needs help here?" he asks.

Jo and I point to each other. We both crack up.

For a moment I forget I'm in the emergency room getting stitches for the gash in my chin. I forget I've been howling and wailing and clutching my jaw ever since I fell and hit it on the coffee table, and Jo had to scoop me up, wrap me in a towel, and rush me to the hospital. I don't forget she held me on her lap the whole way here while my face and eyes throbbed and I cried and bled and screamed bloody murder. I imagined I was dying and my life would go away.

We're laughing now; we're laughing so hard I forget how much it hurt and how scared I am.

✳

Weird. Wow. That was my first memory of being alive. I'd just turned three. I'm fourteen now, but I remember that like it was yesterday. Where was Mom? At work, probably. Or home. She hates hospitals. I don't know why I kept a reminder of that day. All these years, all these reminders. Some things you carry with you forever; you don't need reminders. Some things leave permanent scars.

Mom

"How come Jo never comes with us to Neenee and Poppa's?" I ask.

Mom shifts Beatrice into reverse and doesn't answer. Beatrice is our truck. Jo named it, she says, after a line in an Eminem song: "The streets ain't never want you Beatrice."

At the end of the driveway, Mom digs in her purse for her sunglasses and slides them on, even though it isn't sunny. They hide her red eyes.

"Mom? How come —"

"It's complicated," she says.

But it's Thanksgiving, I think. Jo should be with us. She should come. "What does 'complicated' mean?"

Mom lets out a long sigh. "Oh, Nick," is all she says.

"What's complicated?" I ask again. "What's —"

"Okay! You know that time you broke Zachary's fire engine?"

"It was a accident," I cry. I already explained a hundred times that I was testing the ladder to see if it could reach to the window, because the burning people might have to jump through the window to escape.

Mom tilts her head at me and smiles a little. "I know you didn't do it on purpose. But remember how Zachary's mom wouldn't let you play with him after that?"

I feel sad all over again, remembering. "Why couldn't I play with Zachary? Jo fixed the ladder."

"I know she did."

"And I apologized." I wanted Zachary to be my friend again. I said he could play with all of my toys, all the time. He could even break them and I wouldn't care.

Mom sighs again. "Some people can be very unforgiving."

"What's 'unforgiving'?"

"Nick —"

"Never mind." I know what it means.

We stop at a red light, and Mom grips the steering wheel harder. "It means holding a grudge," she says without looking at me. "It means a person won't give you a second chance. It means you can't drop it and move on, so you exclude people from your life who could be your family — people who want to, who would love to, but you won't let them." She shifts and guns Beatrice.

I think about this. I thought "unforgiving" was not saying I'm sorry and meaning it. "So Zachary's mom holds a grudge on me?"

Mom mutters, "Forget it."

I can't forget it. I don't want to forget it. I want to understand and I want Zachary to be my friend. "Jo says Zachary's mom is a bitch."

"She's not the only one." Mom's jaw clenches.

She reaches over and squeezes my knee. "I'm sorry, sweetie. This has nothing to do with you. Don't say that word again, okay? It's not a nice word."

"It's a dog, right?"

Mom removes her hand.

"Jo says —"

"Can we not talk about Jo? Can we not talk at all?"

A car bolts through the intersection, and Mom has to slam on the brakes to avoid it. She says the F word.

I ball my fist to slug her in the arm four times, wondering if we're going to add "bitch" to our slug scale. It would probably only get one slug, like "damn." Or maybe two, like "shit." I think Mom's not having a very good day already, so I don't slug her. I repeat what Jo always says, "For a price, I'd be willing to forget I ever heard that."

Mom laughs. "You're even starting to sound like Jo."

I smile wide, showing my teeth.

We don't talk the rest of the way to Neenee and Poppa's house. Mom fiddles with the radio until she finds a station with slow, boring music. It makes me sleepy, and I close my eyes.

The next thing I know Poppa is hauling me out of my seat and squeezing me, his scratchy beard scraping against my face. "Hey, Nicholas. How's my best boy?" Poppa sets me down on the sidewalk. At arm's length he examines me. "Look at you. Every time I see you, you've grown another foot."

I glance down at my feet and count, "One. Two." Poppa laughs. He hugs Mom and says, "Hi, honey. We were getting worried about you."

"We got a late start," Mom murmurs. "Sorry." She removes the Jell-O salad from the truck cab. It's still a little watery, but that's because the refrigerator's on the fritz again. There aren't too many miniature marshmallows either, because Jo opened the bag last night. She showed me how to roast mini marshmallows on the stove with a toothpick. She said now I know how to start the house on fire.

"Erin, Nicholas, there you are." Neenee flings open the front screen door. "Come up here and give your grandma a big smooch." She opens her arms to me, and I run.

Neenee is squishy and she smells like almonds. "Hello, Erin." She kisses Mom on the cheek. "You look thin." Her forehead wrinkles. "You okay?"

"I'm fine," Mom says.

Neenee holds Mom's eyes.

"I'm fine."

Neenee shifts to me and grins. "Nicky, look at you. All dressed up in your Sunday go-to-meetin' clothes."

"What's 'go-to-meetin''?" I ask.

Neenee doesn't answer because she's whisking us inside. Uncle Derrick and Aunt Lizzie are already there with their four born losers. That's what Jo calls them. They're all lined up on the couch with their dad, watching football. One of them bares his fangs at me like he's going to eat me alive. He might.

I hang on to Mom for protection. As we pass the bathroom, the toilet flushes, and Aunt Lizzie barrels out. My eyes pop. I want to say what I'm thinking: Wow, you're fat! But I do like Jo tells me when I shouldn't blurt out: I count to myself, One ignoramus, two ignoramus . . .

Mom and Aunt Lizzie and Neenee start gabbing in the kitchen, and I get bored. Poppa and Uncle Derrick are cussing out the ref on TV. My cousins have disappeared, so I wander out to the backyard to see what they're up to.

The oldest two are leaning against the toolshed, smoking cigarettes. "Hey, Nicky," one of them calls. "Want a drag?" He offers me a slimy butt.

I curl a lip. Cancer sticks, that's what Jo calls cigarettes. She made Mom stop smoking so she wouldn't die. I'm just about to inform my cousins that their lungs are black and shriveled when *bam!* A soccer ball clobbers me right in the face, and my glasses go flying.

"Oh, sorry, Nicky." My younger cousin rushes up to me. "I thought with four eyes you'd see it coming." He snickers. They all hee-haw.

My cheek feels like it's on fire and I want to cry, but I don't want my cousins to think I'm a baby. If Jo was here, she'd smack him upside the head. I find my glasses in the grass and put them back on.

My cousin tousles my hair and kicks the soccer ball to my

other cousin. I wait for them to ask me to play, but they don't, so I wander back into the house.

It smells like roasted turkey and gravy and pumpkin pie. I wonder again why Jo hates Thanksgiving.

Mom isn't in the kitchen anymore. Neenee is smashing potatoes and asking Aunt Lizzie how she's feeling. Aunt Lizzie replies, "Like a hippo. If this baby gets any bigger, they're going to need the Jaws of Life to get him out of me." She rubs her big belly. "He's kicking." Aunt Lizzie sees me in the doorway. "Come here, Nicky. You want to feel?"

"No way." It makes my jaw ache just thinking about swallowing a baby. That's how Mom said babies get in there. Jo snorted and said, "Don't believe that, Nick. We'll talk later." But I do believe it. It makes sense.

"Where's Mom?" I ask.

Neenee says, "I think she went to find you. To give you the wishbone. Tell her we're just about ready to eat."

Mom isn't in the living room. She isn't in the basement. I find her outside in Beatrice, listening to her sleepy music. And crying.

I tap on the passenger window.

Mom's head jerks up, and she yanks the keys out of the ignition. She blows her nose in a Kleenex. I sweep a fake fork to my mouth, since I don't think she can hear with the window rolled up.

Mom opens her door and steps down to the street. "Bet you're starving, huh?" She circles around the front of Beatrice.

"Not really," I tell her, because suddenly I'm not hungry. I just want to go home.

I take Mom's hand and squeeze it. She squeezes back. Let's go, I want to say, but Mom pulls me toward the house, smiling, swinging our hands.

At the door we stop, and Mom says, "I almost forgot." She pulls the turkey wishbone out of her front pocket. It's warm and greasy. "Want to make a wish?" She curls an index finger around one end of the bone.

"Not yet," I say. "It has to dry." Mom knows that. The wish won't take unless the bone breaks.

Everybody's seated when we reach the dining room. "There you are." Neenee bustles in from the kitchen, removing her apron. "Hurry up. Take your seats for the blessing."

Mom and I sit down. I notice all the chairs are full. That's not right. There should be an extra place setting on the other side of me. For Jo. My other mom.

Why hasn't anyone even asked where Jo is? The turkey is steaming and there's a lump of butter melting down the sides of the mashed potatoes, and all I can think about is how much I miss Jo. I wonder what she's doing right now. I meet Mom's eyes, her faraway eyes, and I know she's thinking the same thing.

Poppa says, "Lord, we are gathered here today — "

"Wait," I say. "Wait till everybody's here."

All the bowed heads rise in unison. Neenee blinks at me. "What do you mean, Nicky? We *are* all here."

"Jo isn't. We should wait for her."

I see Neenee glance at Mom. Mom closes her eyes and drops her head down. "Jo isn't coming, Nick," Mom says. "You know that."

"But why?" I ask. "We want her here. What's complicated about that?"

Neenee stares at Mom. Mom keeps her head down. Neenee repeats, "You heard your mother. She isn't coming." She says to Poppa, "Say the blessing, Phil."

"I hate you," I blurt out. I say to Neenee, "You're a bitch." I don't know why; it's all confused with complications and forgiveness.

Chairs scrape back. Mom grabs my arm and yanks me toward her, away from Uncle Derrick. He's got my other arm and he's snarling in my face, "You little jerk. Apologize to your grandma."

"No," I snipe at him.

Mom hugs me to her. "I'm sorry. He didn't mean it, Derrick. He doesn't understand."

"Yes, I do." My voice muffles in Mom's bulky sweater.

I feel Mom scoot back and stand up. "I'm sorry," she says. "We'll just go." Mom lifts me, and I wrap my legs around her waist and hug her neck. "Maybe next year . . . " She heads for the door.

"Erin," Neenee calls. "Phil, stop them."

"I'm sorry, Dad," Mom says outside on the porch. "He doesn't understand."

Poppa says, "Then explain it to him."

Mom whispers in my hair, so low I don't think anyone else can hear, "I can't. I don't know how."

*

She never did explain. She never could. She never talked to me about important stuff, vital stuff, when she could have. When she needed to.

I wish . . .

I don't know what I wish. I wish I hadn't saved that stupid wishbone in my scrapbook. But back then, what did I know? I was a stupid little kid.

Jo

"I don't want them to be dead!" I wail.

Mom says, "That's what *happens* when you don't take care of them. When was the last time you *fed* them?"

"I don't know." I hiccup in a sob. "I thought you were feeding them."

"They're *your* fish. They're *your* responsibility." Mom's angry, and I step back out of range. She'd never hit me. She only says, "I guess we don't have to worry about feeding them anymore, do we?" She nets the last dead body from my aquarium while I crumple on the floor and bawl my head off.

"What's going on?" Jo bops into my room. She shoves her hard hat under her armpit. "Whoa, there, Saint Nick. Who died?"

That makes me cry harder.

Mom mutters, "Some saint. He killed his fish."

"I did not!" I scream at Mom. I launch to my feet and rush her; start pounding on her back with my fists.

"Stop that." Jo grabs my wrist and wrenches me away. "Don't you *ever* hit your mother. Don't you ever hit a girl, period. You hear me?" she snarls in my face.

I cower because when Jo's mad, watch out.

"Now tell me what happened," she says more calmly.

Mom answers, "No one bothered to feed the fish. I told you he was too young for pets."

"I am not," I shoot back.

Jo takes a deep breath. "This is my fault. We went over the water temperature and how the fish need oxygen to breathe and how the snails keep the tank clean. But I don't remember talking about how often to feed them. Do you, Nick?"

"No," I lie. Jo told me to sprinkle the food in once a day, every day. I just forgot.

"Sorry, hon," she says to Mom. "It won't happen again."

Jo jabs me on the arm.

Mom murmurs, "No more pets. I can't take them dying." She's talking about Lucky.

Jo swallows hard. "Uh, yeah —"

A howl, then a squealing like a siren makes us all jump. Jo says, "Don't follow me," and sprints for the door.

Mom and I exchange a look. Right. I race after Jo, with Mom on my heels. We run through the kitchen and head to the backyard.

Jo yells, "No! Get back. Back!"

The screen door slams behind me. As I skid to a stop in the grass, a mass of fur comes charging at me, and I scream.

Jo shrieks, "Put him down. Let go!" Jo's beating on this thing, this animal, this hairy beast. All I hear is hissing and squalling, then I see Savage, our cat, drop to the grass. The beast's fangs glisten. Savage tears toward me, and I crouch, covering my head. Mom flings open the screen, and Savage barrels for the basement.

Jo hollers, "Is he okay?"

Mom doesn't answer. I say, "I think so." I didn't see any limping or shredded skin.

Mom glares at Jo. "What the hell is that?"

I bound over and slug Mom once for "hell."

Jo hooks her fingers around something on the beast. A collar. The beast is a dog. A monster dog.

"She likes cats," Jo says. "She was just playing with Savage."

"Oh, that's comforting." Mom expels a puff of air. "Where'd it come from?" She folds her arms tight across her chest. Meanwhile, I slowly approach the dog. "Be careful, Nick." Mom thrusts out a hand to snag my shirt, but misses.

Jo says, "Sit," and stiff-arms the dog. The dog obeys. "I brought her home from work."

Mom goes, "Jo —"

"She won't hurt Nick. She's been hanging around the construction site the last couple of weeks. I think someone dumped her. She's starving, Erin. A couple of us have been feeding her, then today the big dope chases the forklift and gets her leg caught in the rigging. It looks pretty mangled. I couldn't just leave her out there."

I pet the dog's head, and she licks my chin.

Mom and Jo fix on each other for a long minute before Mom drops her head and shakes it. She pivots and returns inside. Jo and I grimace at each other. We hear Mom clomp on the stairs, and we trail behind.

"Stay," Jo orders the dog.

"She's a sweet dog, hon," Jo says at Mom's back. "Someone trained her. She knows 'sit' and 'shake.' Did you see how fast she dropped Savage after I told her no? She's really gentle; she'll be great with Nick."

"No more animals, Jo," Mom's voice carries in the basement. "Especially not a dog. You know I can't go through that again." She inhales a deep, shaky breath, and lets it out. "Nick's too young to be responsible, and I'm the one who ends up taking care of the pets. Have you noticed that?" She stops at the bottom of the stairs and twists around. "Either of you?" We almost plow into her.

"What about Savage?" I say.

Mom narrows her eyes at me.

Jo whispers in my ear, "Smartass." I slug her once for "ass."

Mom's the one who let Savage in one night. He was a stray. She's the one who named him.

She claps her hands and clicks her tongue. "S-a-a-vage. Come on, baby. Where are you? You're okay."

Jo sits on the step next to me. "She's really cool, Nick. A Great Pyrenees, one of the guys said. We could breed her and have puppies."

I widen my eyes at Jo.

"Okay, that's probably not my most brilliant idea at the moment." There's a scuffling noise at the far edge of the basement, behind a boxful of old toys and Jo's busted stereo. Savage shoots up the wall to the ceiling joists, and growls.

Mom coos, "It's okay, baby. Calm down."

Savage skulks away toward the furnace. He's feral, a wildcat. Mom called Jo the same thing once. Jo said, "Yeah, and you're the only one who can tame me." It must be true, because Mom's the only one Savage will let near him. Mom kisses and clicks and eventually coaxes Savage into her arms.

As she hurries toward us, Jo and I jump up and separate to let Mom by.

Jo bends over to give me a pony ride up the stairs. On the way she says, "You know, Nick, everything happens for a reason. Lucky gets killed, and lo and behold, this dog shows up. I think she was sent here to fill up the hole in our hearts left by Lucky. Especially your mom's."

I don't remember all that much about Lucky. We only had her a couple of months before she got run over by a car. I was the one who left the gate open the morning Lucky got out. She ran straight for Mom. She was still a puppy. Mom was already in the car, backing out of the garage. She swore it wasn't my fault, that she wasn't looking, but I still hear the squeal and feel sick all over again.

Now, Jo lowers me to the landing and stands with her hand pressed flat against my chest. She's staring out the back door, where Mom is sitting on the grass with the dog's head in her lap. Savage is hunched on top of the shed, growling. Mom's running her fingers down the dog's front leg. The skin's all ripped and bloodied, and a length of bone is exposed. Mom hugs the dog's head and starts to rock her. She must notice us at the screen, because she says, "Call around for a vet. See if anyone can get us in right away."

Jo balls a fist and holds it out to me for a knuckle knock. She says softly, "Everything for a reason."

✳

Our new dog ended up having to get her front leg amputated. We named her Lucky 2. While the vet was discussing the operation with Mom, Jo snuck out the film. It's cool, the X-ray of Lucky 2's busted leg. I still have it in my scrapbook (not the leg).

Jo said, "You get a lot of extra body parts, Nick. Parts you don't need to stay alive. You really only need one of everything."

"Yeah?" I quipped. "So how come I got two moms?"

Jo was quick. "One to bring you into this world, and one to take you out." She laughed at my expression. If I knew then what I know now, I might've answered, "Wrong. You only need one for that too."

Mom and Jo

I slam through the front door. Jo must be home already, because the CD player is blasting through the house with the bass turned up so loud the dirty dishes in the kitchen sink are rattling. Mad as I am, I catch a whiff of Mom's smelly soap. Her laugh reaches my ears and I think, Good, they're both here.

The bathroom door is closed, but I don't care. I burst in. "Why did you do this to me?" I scream.

Jo says, "Geezus, Nick. Ever heard of knocking?" She and Mom, who are both in the bathtub naked, slide down below the bubbles so I can't see them. Like I never have. They take baths together all the time. I used to bathe with them until I got too big.

Jo raises a bubbly arm. "Is school out already? What time is it?"

"I hate you! I hate both of you." I slam the door in their stupid ugly faces.

Out in the backyard, I find Lucky 2's chewed-up football and fling it as far as I can. She scrambles to her feet and hobbles over to retrieve it. I throw it again. She brings it back. I throw it again. She brings it back. The next throw I make sure she has to weave around the wheelbarrow and the soccer net, then clamber over the rock wall into Mom's strawberry patch. Lucky 2's wheezing and foaming at the mouth as she drops the football at my feet. Just as I'm about to launch it again, Jo wrenches it away from me.

"Stop torturing her," she says, flames shooting from her eyes. "What is wrong with you?" She slams the football to the grass, where Lucky 2 paws it and collapses with a moan.

Mom comes out the back door, her hair soaked and stringy. She's got a robe on and she pulls the belt tighter. The expression on her face is half worry, half mad.

I kick the leg of the picnic table and mutter, "I hate you."

Jo grips my arm hard. "Don't you *ever* say that. Don't you ever say that to either of us, you hear? We do *not* hate in this house. Now what's this about? What happened?"

I whirl on them. "You're freaks. That's what. Everybody says so. And you made me a freak too." My face burns like it did at school. I was just playing trucks in the dirt with Matthew, minding my own business, when those big guys showed up at the kindergarten fence.

"Hey, Nick," one of them called to me. "Come over here. We want to ask you a question."

I ignored them.

"Come on, Nick. It's an easy question."

Matthew said, "You know those guys?"

"No," I replied. But I had a bad feeling.

"Nick!"

Matthew told me, "Just go see what they want so they'll shut up. I'll come with you." We both got up and brushed off our pants.

When we were a foot away from the fence, one of the guys curled his fingers around the chain link, smiled, and said, "So, Nick, we were wondering . . . " He couldn't finish because he was laughing. What was so funny? Another one went, "We were wondering if you had a dick." They all sniggered.

I knew he was trying to trick me, so I said, "No."

The first kid arched his eyebrows and sobered up fast. "You don't have a dick, Nick?" He turned to his buddies. "Nick doesn't have a dick."

They were howling now. Matthew whispered in my ear that a dick means a penis. I felt stupid and shouted at those guys, "I mean, yeah, I do."

The serious guy said, "Are you sure? Maybe you should check."

Matthew grabbed my sleeve and tugged. "Let's go. They're being nasty." Over our shoulders, he sniped, "I'm going to tell Mr. H you guys are perverts."

That made them laugh louder. "Ooh, we're real scared." The serious guy smashed his face against the fence, glaring at me. He snarled, "Especially since the real pervert is your mom, Nick. Or should I say *moms*."

My whole body froze. I tried to speak, but couldn't. I wanted to say something, yell at them, charge, beat the fence so they would go away.

The guy's eyes bored into mine. "That's right, Nicky," he went. "Your moms are freaks. And so are you. Dickless Nicholas. Hey, that's a good one." He elbowed his buddy to the left. "Dickless Nicholas." They both fell to the ground laughing. The guy cupped his hands around his mouth and hollered across the playground, "Dickless Nicholas," indicating me. They all took up the chant: "Dickless Nicholas. Dickless Nicholas."

I ran into the classroom and hid in the closet.

Jo is looking at me funny. "Why did you have to be this way?" I yell at Mom and Jo. "Why did you have to have me?"

Mom's face drains of color, like I stuck a knife in her belly. I don't care. How does she think I feel?

Jo clamps a hand over my shoulder. "What happened, Nick? Tell us."

I shake loose from her grasp. I want to tell, but I can't with Mom standing there. She might cry.

The phone rings in the house, and Jo says, "That better be the school."

Mom murmurs, "I'll get it." She heads for the house.

Jo looks at me. "Well?"

"What's a pervert?" I ask.

Jo's jaw clenches. She lowers herself to the picnic bench and pulls me close to her. "Did somebody call you that?"

"No. They called *you* that."

Her face hardens.

"They called me Dickless Nicholas."

Jo sucks in her lips, but can't hide her grin. "Oh, Nick." She tries to hug me, but I push her away. "Come on," she says, "it's kind of funny."

"No, it's not!" I scream at her.

"Okay, I'm sorry." She grabs my wrist and hangs on.

I'm afraid I might burst into tears, and I don't want to. I'm not a baby.

"They're just words, Nick. They can't hurt you."

She's wrong. They hurt plenty. On the inside, where you can't see the gash. Where you can't stitch it up and the scar doesn't show. But the hurt doesn't go away because the words keep cutting and reopening the wound. Pervert. Pervert.

"So call them something back," Jo says. "Like fartface. Or boogerbrain."

I smile a little. "Mucous membrane," I suggest.

Jo makes a face. "You watch too much Discovery Channel." She stands and tousles my hair. "I need a drink. How 'bout you?"

"Where's my dad?" I blurt. Those guys made me wonder again.

That makes Jo stop. "You don't have one," she says.

"Why?"

Jo considers that for a minute. "Why is the world round?" she asks.

"Because it is."

"Right. It is what it is. Now I really need a drink."

"Make mine a double," I say.

Jo smirks. "Don't let your mom hear that." She bends over to give me a pony ride. I think I'm too big, but I jump on her back anyway.

Mom's hanging up the phone as we gallop into the kitchen. Jo drops me in the window seat and heads for the fridge. "Mr. Hasselback got Matthew to tell him what happened," Mom says. Her eyes meet mine and she looks . . . sad. Helpless. "They have a pretty good idea who did it — these fifth graders who've been harassing the little kids lately. Mr. H wants to talk to his kids, but he's not sure what to tell them. Or how. He wants to know what we want him to do."

"Tell them the truth," Jo says.

"No!" I cry.

Jo shuts the fridge and tosses me a Coke. She pops the top on her beer.

Mom says, "You've already had two."

Jo mutters, "But who's counting?"

Mom sighs.

Jo glugs. She swipes her mouth and says, "So, what'd you tell Mr. H?" She leans against the kitchen counter.

"I told him we'd get back to him." Mom scrapes out a chair and sits at the table. Jo loops a leg over the chair cattycorner from her. She drinks her beer, wiggling her eyebrows at me. Mom must've switched off the CD player before answering the phone, because it's quiet. Too quiet.

She winds a strand of damp hair behind her ear and says softly, "I told you this would happen."

Jo goes, "And I told you we'd deal with it. Nick" — she twists to face me — "you have two moms."

"Duh," I say.

She cricks a lip. "You know we're gay, right?"

I roll my eyes.

"And you know what 'gay' means, right?"

Mom cuts in, "He's only five, Jo."

"Five and three-quarters," I say.

"He understands." Jo tips her beer. She swallows. "You know your mom and I love each other, right? And we love you. That doesn't make us perverts. That makes us happy and it makes you lucky to have so much love in your life."

"Yeah, right," I mumble. "I'm so lucky." I study my shoes. There's a drawing of Lucky 2 on the left sneaker. I did it with Magic Marker this morning. I'd started to draw my new fish on the other shoe, but art time ended.

"Nick!"

I flinch. "What?"

Jo widens her eyes at Mom. "Forget it, Jo," Mom says. "He's not ready."

"Yes, I am," I tell her. "I know I don't have a dad. Kenny DiPoto doesn't have a dad either because his dad got knifed in jail."

"Geezus," Jo breathes. "What kind of neighborhood is this?"

Mom's still staring at me. "Go on," she says. "What else do you know?"

I pick out a chunk of mud from my tread and flick it on the floor. "Lots of kids don't have dads. Nobody else has two moms."

"See how lucky you are? Double the pleasure, double the fun." Jo swigs the rest of her beer. She chucks the empty can over Mom's head into the trash, then heads to the fridge for another.

I sip my Coke.

"Just because nobody else in your class has two moms doesn't make it bad," Mom informs me. "Or wrong. It means you're different. It means you're special."

"Yeah, right," I mumble again. Dickless Nicholas. That's so special.

Jo pops the top on her can, and foam oozes out the drinking hole. She sucks it up fast.

"Look," Jo says, setting her can down hard on the table and swinging into her chair, "if you want, you can tell the kids you have a dad. His name is Joe."

"No," Mom says, louder than she needs to. "We promised we'd never do that. We wouldn't lie."

"So, what?" Jo says. "We just ignore it? We don't talk about it?"

Mom's eyes fuse to Jo's beer can. "I didn't say that."

"He's going to have to learn how to fight, Erin. To defend himself. Because this is just the beginning. Even if we're open and honest, he's going to have to live in the real world. You know that."

"No fighting." Mom repeats it to me, "No fighting."

Jo tells her, "I had to fight. Every day of my life I had to fight."

"Nick isn't you," Mom snaps. Her face changes, and she swallows hard. "There are other ways."

"Sure," Jo says. "Ignore it. Turn the other cheek. Let everyone use you as a punching bag. Then it kills you from the inside. They get you coming and going, Erin." She takes a long draw on her beer.

This talk is scaring me.

Mom turns and blinks at me. "I'm sorry, Nick. I'm sorry we did this to you."

"We didn't do anything to him," Jo snarls. "We gave him life and love. A happy home and a loving family. He has everything. Everything that counts."

"I don't have Xbox," I say. "Matthew has Xbox."

Jo and Mom pause a beat. Their eyes meet, and they crack up. I think — hope — that means they'll get me Xbox. Jo reaches out and places her hand over Mom's on the table. Mom takes a deep breath. Jo lifts Mom's hand and kisses it. "What do we want Nick's teacher to do?" Mom asks.

Jo says, "Nick, what do you want to do?"

I don't even have to think about it. "Find those kids and kill them."

Jo shrugs at Mom. "That works for me."

*

Nobody got beat up. Not that time, anyway. Jo went to school with me every day for a week, though, and stood at the fence. I'd see her out the window during art, story time, snack time. She'd be posing, posturing like a tough guy. Yeah, Jo's real tough.

What you see on the outside isn't always what you get on the inside, especially with girls. I learned that the hard way.

Mom

Jo sticks out her tongue at me. It's covered with chewed-up Fritos. Gross-out contest, but I don't have anything to eat. I twist my finger up my nose and pretend to eat my boogers. Mom slams in the back door from the garage. "Turn down that damn CD!" she hollers.

Jo widens her eyes at me. I shrink in my chair. Jo jumps off the counter where she's been sitting and charges for the living room.

I clench my fist to slug Mom once for saying "damn," but only out of habit. We abandoned the slug system a while ago. Jo said she didn't want to encourage me to hit girls, but I think it's because she got slugged the most.

At the kitchen table, I'm practicing handwriting my name for school: Nicholas Nathaniel Thomas Tyler. It takes two lines to write it all.

Mom unzips her parka and presses my head to her stomach. "Hi, honey." She takes a deep, calming breath. Her hand is freezing on my neck, and her zipper digs into my ear. "That looks nice," she says.

"How come I have four first names?" I ask.

Jo pads back to the kitchen in her grizzly bear slippers. Mom and I got them for her birthday last week and she wears them all the time. "We couldn't decide on a name for you," Jo answers. "You almost got named Lucky, since you took on the first try." She smirks at Mom. Mom shoots Jo a warning look. I think Mom's afraid I'm going to ask what that means, but I don't. Jo takes Mom's coat and kisses her, while I continue to write my name.

Jo says to Mom, "Another shitty day at the office?"

Mom sighs heavily. "I hate this job. All I do is input orders and print invoices. It's mindless. It's so boring I could scream."

"Go ahead." Jo claps her hands over my ears. Her hands are rough and dry, but warm. She leans over and says upside down in my face, "If the neighbor's ask, tell them we're having wild sex parties over here."

I stick my pencil up Jo's nose.

Mom slumps into the seat beside me. She rubs her eyes with her knuckles and smears her mascara.

Jo says, "So quit." She shuffles off to the living room to hang up Mom's coat.

"Sure," Mom says under her breath. "Quit. Like I could." She calls to Jo, "There's something wrong with the car again. It's idling rough and it almost died at the light. The brakes feel funny, like they're not catching. I couldn't tell for sure. The roads are pure ice."

Jo shuffles back. "Okay, I'll look at it tomorrow. You can take Beatrice."

Mom flips through the mail. "Don't you need to drive?"

Jo heads for the fridge.

I sense the tension even before I look up. Mom's staring at Jo's back. "Don't tell me."

Jo grabs a beer and shuts the fridge. "If you insist."

"You didn't."

She pops the top.

"Jo."

"They gave the promotion to that jerk-off Jerry Vigil. The guy operates a backhoe like he's driving the Indy 500. He's an asshole. Pardon my French." She winks at me.

Mom slaps down the wad of bills. "So you just quit?"

"What did you want me to do? Stay and take that shit? They never promote *the girls*." She swigs her beer and licks the foam off her upper lip. "I'd be an Operator One the rest of my life."

Mom pinches the bridge of her nose, the way she does when she's got a headache. "That was a good job, Jo," she says weakly. "Steady, at least. Good money, and we need it." She gets up and goes to the sink. Cranking on the faucet, she pours herself a glass of water and reaches up to the shelf for the bottle of Excedrin. "That's the third job you've had in the last six months." She knocks back a couple of pills.

"But who's counting?" Jo rolls her eyes at me.

"It's actually the fourth," I say, "if you count getting fired from CopyMax."

"Which we do not." Jo slit-eyes me. She scoops up a handful of Fritos and tosses them into her mouth.

I try to keep a straight face, but it's hard when I add, "Fired for copying your naked butt and gluing it on your boss's chair."

"Hey." Jo clamps a hand over my mouth. "How'd you know about that?" She spins and holds up both palms to Mom. "I did not show him the picture, I swear."

I finish the fourth Nicholas Nathaniel Thomas Tyler at the bottom of the page and rip the sheet out of my writing tablet. "I know everything that goes on around here." I wiggle my eyebrows up at Jo. "I'm Invisible Boy."

Jo snorts. "If Invisible Boy didn't eat like Solid Waste King, I wouldn't have to work at all."

I say to Mom, "At least Jo didn't get fired this time."

Mom expels a weary breath. "What are we having for dinner?"

Jo says, "Fritos."

It's a joke, but Mom explodes. "Why do I have to do everything around here? I'm sick of this."

Jo and I both jump.

Mom storms over to the cupboard and yanks open the door. "I work, I cook, I clean." She slams the door. "Did either of you even *think* to feed Lucky 2 and Savage? Did you feed your fish?"

Jo and I look at each other. Did we?

"Which reminds me" — Mom storms to the pantry — "your room stinks to high heaven, Nick. When was the last time you cleaned your tank?"

I shrug. I don't remember.

Lucky 2 hears Mom open the cupboard and scrabbles to her feet from under the table. The odor reaches me and Jo at the same time. We both go, "Ew," and plug our noses.

Jo says, in a nasally voice, "I think we should stop feeding Lucky 2 that cheap dog food. A little heavy on the horse meat, if you catch my drift."

Jo and I fan our faces. I say, "We could put Beano in her water. That's what Matthew's mom does for his dad."

Jo laughs.

Mom doesn't. "Yeah, we could," she snipes. "If Lucky 2 *had* any water."

I see Lucky 2's water dish is dry again and wince at Jo.

Mom kicks shut the pantry door. "I've had it!" she yells. "You have *no* respect for me, either one of you. You're irresponsible. You're undependable. I have to do everything for everybody and I'm sick of it. Do you hear me?" She's looking right at me when she adds, "You're *useless*."

The force of her voice — the word — I feel like bursting into tears.

Mom stalks off toward the bedroom and slams the door. The whole house shakes.

"Geez," Jo says, popping a Frito into her mouth. "Who shoved a burr up her butt?"

I'd laugh, but I'm still reeling from Mom's anger. Her . . . evaluation of me.

"Okay" — Jo extends an arm — "give me the crash helmet. I'm going in."

From the middle of the table I shove Jo's hard hat over. She smooshes it onto her frizzy hair and, as she's rolling up her sleeves, says, "I suggest you clear out, Nick. This could get ugly."

I collect my papers and Coke and head to my room. Mom's right about the stench. I decide to surprise her by cleaning my aquarium. Even though the bathroom separates our bedrooms, I hear Mom's raised voice: "You *know* I wanted to go back to school next semester, Jo. I can't stand feeling trapped in this data entry job. I'm going brain-dead."

Jo calmly replies, "No one's making you stay there, Erin."

"You are!" Mom shouts. "I never know if we'll have enough money to cover all the bills, let alone save anything for my college."

"So apply for a scholarship. You're smart enough. Don't put this off on me. You're always doing that —

"Erin, come back here. Don't walk away from me.

"Erin!"

I try to concentrate on other things, like transferring my fish to a bowl of water. I insert my earplugs from my portable CD player and turn up the volume full blast. As I net the last tetra, a loud *clunk* on Mom and Jo's bedroom door makes me cower. I remove one earplug.

Jo yells, "Goddammit. I hate when you do this. If you want to fight, let's fight."

I stick it back in. The way Jo showed me, I get the bucket

and drain all the water from the tank. I swipe the algae off the glass. I fill the tank back up and carefully ladle in my fish. The house feels calmer now. I climb into bed and cover my head with the pillow. I turn down the volume on my player so I don't get another earache.

Even with the echoes of Jo's shouting and stomping around and the music in my ears and the wind howling outside my bedroom window, I feel myself drifting off.

Next thing I know someone's shaking my shoulder. My eyelids flutter.

"Nick?" Mom is perched on my bed, stroking my hair. "Sweetie? I brought you some dinner. Chicken nuggets and creamed corn — your favorite."

I sit up, remove the one earplug that didn't fall out. Mom poises a TV tray over my lap and burrows in under the covers. The smell of chicken makes my mouth water.

"Where's Jo?" I ask, scraping my eyes.

Mom hands me my glasses. I forgot to take them off again and they slid down the pillow. Mom answers, "She went out."

"In the blizzard? She'll freeze to death." Jo hates the cold. Plus, if the roads are icy like Mom said . . .

I think about how fast Jo drives and how she weaves in and out of traffic and hotdogs all over the place. A vision of her in Beatrice, crashed in a ditch, frozen and bleeding, makes me shiver and whimper.

"Don't worry." Mom slips an arm in under my shoulders and snuggles up to me. "Jo can take care of herself."

I'm not so sure about that.

"Come on, eat this gourmet meal I brewed up in my cauldron. If you don't, I'll turn you into a frog. Ribbit." She pokes my ribs.

Even though my stomach feels queasy, I pick up a chicken nugget and swirl it in the corn. I offer it to Mom. She declines, so I bite off the end.

Mom hugs my head to her. "I didn't mean it about you being useless," she says. "You're the most precious thing in life to me. I'm sorry. I lost my temper."

"Did you look in your armpit?"

"What?" Mom wrinkles her nose.

"That's where Jo always finds hers."

Mom smiles and shakes her head. I smile too, because I made Mom happy.

"I cleaned my aquarium," I tell her. So she wouldn't think I was totally useless.

"Thank you." She rests her chin on my head. "You're my pride and joy, Nicholas Nathaniel Thomas Tyler. The day you were born was the happiest day of my life."

"I know," I say. Jo told me. The happiest day of both their lives. "Promise we'll always be together?"

Mom tilts her head down to meet my eyes. "Are you worried about that? Because you shouldn't worry. Married people fight. It's normal. It doesn't mean we don't love each other, or you. It doesn't mean anything. Okay?"

"Okay," I say, "but do you promise?"

"Cross my heart and hope to die." She crisscrosses her heart with her finger.

A ribbon of warmth weaves through me. I'm not really

worried. Jo's already promised me a hundred million times. The Three Mouseketeers, she calls us. All for one and one for all. "A promise is a vow, Nick," she tells me. "It's a bond of trust between two people." She says if you can't trust another person, you have nothing between you. No glue; nothing binding you. She tells me, "You can trust me when I make a promise to you. It sticks." She presses my hand to her heart and holds it.

I trust her. I trust Mom too. The bond of trust between us is permanent.

✳

Sometimes I wish Mom and I had never had that conversation, or that I didn't remember it so vividly. The chicken nuggets. The feel of Mom's chin on my head. So much talk about promises. That's all it was — talk. But when you're a little kid you need to hear it. You fear the worst. You want to believe that your life will be good and nothing will change and everything — everyone — goes on forever. It's not until later that you find out people are liars and forever is a myth and the glue is only as good as the two ends it holds together.

Mom and Jo

I hate my third grade teacher. I'm not supposed to say "hate,"
but when it comes to Mrs. Ivey, "hate" is the only word.

The second week of school she made me move my desk
out to the hall during math because I was being a disruption.
Mom asked, "What were you doing?" I told her, "Joking
around with Matthew." We got our subtraction review done
early and didn't feel like putting our heads on our desks, so
we drew this picture of Mrs. Ivey with a big hairy wart on
her nose. Jo laughed, but Mom said, "Did Mrs. Ivey see the
picture?"

"Yeah. She took it away."

Mom looked crushed. "You hurt Mrs. Ivey's feelings, Nick.
Did you ever think about that?"

I do think about it. I think about it all night. I decide to be
nicer. It's hard, though. Mrs. Ivey hates me as much as I
hate her.

Friday is parents' night. I don't give Mom and Jo the flyer because I don't want them to go. Somehow they find out. They make me get dressed up. Jo wears her jeans without the shredded butt, and Mom puts on her silky flowered dress with sandals. As Neenee would say, "Sunday go-to-meetin' clothes."

It's not Sunday. When we walk in the front door, I see the teachers have been busy. The halls are decorated with art and writing and social studies projects. The principal, Ms. Gault, greets us and says, "Help yourself to punch and cookies." Not too many parents have shown up. I wish mine hadn't.

Ms. Gault knows me. On Monday I got sent to the principal's office. I warned Mrs. Ivey not to put cichlids in the aquarium, that they'd kill the other fish. They're aggressive and territorial. But she didn't listen. When I called her a murderer, she clenched both my wrists — hard. My first instinct was to defend myself, the way I was taught. I didn't mean to kick her. Honestly. I'd never hurt a girl on purpose. It was just . . . reflex.

Ms. Gault lectured me about acting out and inappropriate behavior in school. When she called home, she got Jo.

I thought I'd be in deep shit that night, but Jo only said, "For a price, I'd be willing to forget I ever heard about this."

"Deal." If Mom found out, she'd make me quit kickboxing.

The price was shoveling Lucky 2's dog poop for a month. It was worth it.

Mom and Ms. Gault's conversation is cut short by the arrival of Matthew and his parents. "Yo, Nick," he calls to me.

I leave my cup and half-eaten cookie on the refreshment table.

Mom and Jo know Matthew's parents. Sometimes I go to his house after school when Mom has classes and Jo works the dinner shift at Denny's. Jo keeps telling me she's going to quit waitressing because it's not a true test of her talents. But she lost her heavy equipment operator's license after she got caught driving drunk on the job. She and Mom had a blowout over that. Well, Jo blew. Mom went to bed. Mom didn't talk to Jo for three whole days. On the fourth day, Mom told me, "Ask Jo to take out the garbage."

Jo said, "Tell your mom she makes me feel like garbage when she treats me this way."

I like going to Matthew's. His mom makes us banana-and-peanut-butter sandwiches, which I tried to teach Jo how to make, but she's allergic to cooking. The only problem is Matthew's mom doesn't allow pets, so Matthew couldn't keep the fish I gave him. Matthew has a new baby sister, Quinn. I asked Mom if I could have a brother or sister, but she said it was too expensive. I said, "I don't mean buy one. Have one." Mom said, "We'll talk about this later."

Jo said I should be careful what I ask for. She said babies are sort of like men: They're fun to play with, but you wouldn't want to bring one home.

"Hey, look." Matthew points over my shoulder. "Our pictures are up."

The main case by the principal's office has our class drawings on display.

I grab Jo's sweatshirt and say, "Wait'll you see this."

Matthew taps the glass. "There's my picture. Hey, Dad," he calls. Matthew whispers in my ear, "Thanks for helping me draw the faces."

"No problem." His picture is matted and pinned up in the center, right underneath the title: "My Family."

Quinn lets out a little whimper, and Mom asks if she can hold the baby. As Matthew's mom hands her over, Jo asks me, "Where's your picture, Nick?"

I scan the display. "I don't know."

Matthew's dad says, "Maybe they didn't have space for all of them in the case." He glances behind us. "There's art on all the walls. It's probably around here somewhere."

Matthew's dad and Jo head off toward B wing, where our classroom is located. Matthew catches up, but I lag behind. They're discussing the game on Sunday. Matthew's going to be a professional football player when he grows up. That or a marine. I'm going to be an ichthyologist, a fish scientist. Or an artist.

Mom shifts the baby to one arm and takes my hand, or tries to. I don't need my mom holding my hand. Not in school.

I hang back. Our family pictures line one wall, and I study each one. Some kids have three or four brothers or sisters, and I think how fun that'd be. I wonder if I'd have to share my bedroom, though, since we only have the two. What if Mom or Jo liked the baby better than me? In lots of kids' pictures there's only one parent. Maybe I should be glad I'm the only kid, with my two moms.

We reach my classroom, and Jo turns around. "Did you see your picture?"

"No," I say.

"Hello, welcome." Mrs. Ivey bustles to the door to meet us. She shakes hands with Matthew's mom and dad. Mom gives the baby back to Matthew's mother and smiles at Mrs. Ivey. "Hi," Mom says.

Mrs. Ivey pretends Mom isn't there. It's the same thing she does to me. I see Jo narrow her eyes, and I get a bad feeling. I want to go home.

Mrs. Ivey chitters away with Matthew's parents, telling them what a pleasure it is to have Matthew in class, what a good student he is. Which is a lie. Matthew's always screwing around.

Before I can think how to stop them, Mom and Jo wander into the room. Mom pauses at the cork bulletin board in back, where our penmanship papers are stapled up. "Here you are." Mom points to my paper.

I beam because I got a B-plus.

Jo says, "Why'd you get a B? What's wrong with your writing?"

"B-plus," I correct her.

Jo frowns at Mom. "Do you see anything wrong with his writing?"

Mom studies the page. "Maybe they weren't supposed to do cursive. None of the other kids are writing in cursive."

"I'm the only one who knows how," I inform her.

Mom examines the other papers. "Nick's letters are a little crooked, I guess."

"Get real." Jo huffs. "Look at these. Half these kids can't even stay in the lines." She spreads a hand under the page next to mine. "The B is backward and so's the D. This kid's, like, totally dyslexic, and she gives her an A-minus."

I want to warn Jo to lower her voice or we'll get busted. Mrs. Ivey is glaring at us.

"Where's your desk?" Mom asks me.

"Right here." I run my hand along the top of my chair.

Jo says, "Clear back here? Didn't you give your teacher our note about sitting you up front because of your vision problems?"

"Yeah. I like sitting in back." Which is true, even if it is hard to see.

I feel Jo's fire. I get a bad feeling. Jo snarls at Mom, "What is this crap?"

It's time to go — now.

Jo stomps past my desk, but Mom lunges out and catches her arm. "Jo, don't."

"Don't what? Make trouble? You haven't seen trouble —"

"Please," Mom pleads.

Please, I plead. Please. I want to clench both their wrists and drag them out of there. I want to go home. Pop popcorn. Roast mini marshmallows over the stove.

Jo pries Mom's fingers off her arm and marches to the front of the room. Mom shakes her head at me. Stop her, I want to scream. Say something! "Excuse me," Jo's voice carries. She fakes a smile at Matthew's mom, then Mrs. Ivey. They stop cooing over Quinn. "Think we could get a little airtime here?"

Matthew's mom steps away, covering the baby's head with her blanket. "Sorry, Jo. Nice to see you again," she says to

Mrs. Ivey. "We appreciate everything you do. We know Matthew's a handful." She grimaces at Matthew's dad.

Jo turns on Mrs. Ivey. "Where's Nick's family picture?" she demands.

Mrs. Ivey's face flushes. "I'm sure it's up." Her voice sounds funny, sort of high and strangled.

"I'm sure it's not," Jo replies.

Mom clutches my hand and heads for the front. No, I think. No. Let's just *go*.

Mrs. Ivey inches backward, away from Jo. Mom extends her other hand. "Hi. I'm Erin Tyler, Nick's mom," she says nicely. "We met the first day of school. You probably don't remember. It was kind of crazy."

"Of course I remember." Mrs. Ivey plasters on her fake smile and shakes Mom's hand.

"Then you remember me too. Nick's other mom?" Jo doesn't extend her hand.

Mrs. Ivey's smile freezes. "Of course."

Jo says to me, "Nick, did you draw a picture of your family?"

I don't answer.

"Nick?"

I swallow hard, and nod.

"And did you see it hanging up?"

My chest hurts. I shake my head.

Mom exhales a long breath, and I know it's meant for Jo. Jo cocks her head at Mrs. Ivey. "Where's Nick's picture?"

Mrs. Ivey's face jiggles. "I . . . I must've missed it. Let me look through my desk." She circles the desk and starts sifting through a stack of papers. "I was in a rush to get everyone's work up and I wanted to show a sampling of all the things we've been doing. You did see his penmanship paper." She glances up briefly. When Jo doesn't reply, Mrs. Ivey adds, "This desk is a disaster. I never have figured out how to stay organized."

Her desk looks extra neat to me. She made all of us clean our desks earlier today.

Jo asks, "How long have you been teaching?"

"Eighteen years," Mrs. Ivey answers.

Jo goes, "Huh. You'd think you'd have a system by now."

I feel Mom send a silent signal to Jo: Stop it. I send one too: Let's leave. Finally, in the bottom drawer, Mrs. Ivey finds my sheet of white construction paper and pulls it out. "For heaven's sake, I don't know how it got down there. I must've misfiled it."

Jo takes the picture from Mrs. Ivey. Her eyes soften and a slow smile spreads across her lips. "Nick," she breathes, "this is . . . Erin, look at this." She passes my picture to Mom.

Mom's eyes widen and her lips part. "Oh my God. Nick, did you draw this?"

"No," Jo answers. "He hired Michelangelo."

I click my tongue. "No, sir."

Jo takes the picture back from Mom. "It's awesome. It's amazing."

I feel warm inside. Happy. I know it's the best picture I ever drew. "That's Lucky 2 and Savage." I indicate to Mom.

"Who's this?" Jo's index finger circles around the clouds.

"That's Lucky and all my fish who died. I figured they

were still family, even though they're in heaven." Completing the cycle of nature, as Jo says.

Mom and Jo look at each other, and Mom's eyes pool with tears. Jo slips an arm around her shoulders. They continue to admire my drawing. I especially like how I drew Mom and Jo, hugging each other. With me squished between them.

Mom says, "I love this, Nick. Can I have it?"

"Yeah," I answer. I drew it for them. I hope Mom sticks it on the refrigerator with all my other drawings.

Mom asks Mrs. Ivey, "Can we take this home tonight?"

"Oh yes."

"Oh no." Jo whips the paper away. "This is too good. I think it deserves to be up front in the main display case." She heads for the door. "Why don't we ask the principal what she thinks?" Stopping in the doorway, Jo turns. "I want Nick to move his desk to the front next to his best friend, Matthew. Since Matthew's such an angel, maybe his good behavior will rub off on Nick." Jo slit-eyes Mrs. Ivey, like, You got a problem with that?

Mrs. Ivey's lips purse. "Whatever you want. You're his parents."

Jo exaggerates a thin smile. She adds, "Since Nick seems to forget to bring home his papers, I'll stop by on Fridays to pick them up. We can discuss his grades."

Mrs. Ivey opens her mouth to say something, then shuts it. I think she's counting to herself: One ignoramus, two . . .

Mom and I catch up with Jo at the end of the hallway. Mom snarls, "Dammit, Jo. Why do you have to be such a bitch? We could've just transferred Nick to the other third grade class."

"She's the bitch," Jo says. "She's the biggest homophobe I've ever met — besides your parents."

Mom seethes, "Don't go there."

Jo adds, looking at me, "We're not giving in and we're not giving up. We're going to stay and fight. Right, Nick?" She balls a fist and holds it out to me. I give her a weak knuckle knock. I don't want to fight.

Mom says, "All you're going to do is give her a reason to hate us. You'll just justify her homophobia."

Jo shakes her head. "You're wrong, Erin. People like that don't need a reason to hate. It comes naturally. And I don't give a shit if she hates us, but to take it out on our kid . . ." Jo glances back over her shoulder at my classroom. "I'll never forgive her. Never."

Mom says, "*That* I believe."

✳

I'm not sure I understood at the time. I understood hate, and still do. But who was right and who was wrong? Whose approach works best? Especially with people like Mrs. Ivey, and the world is full of them, I'm learning. You can't fight them all. After parents' night I started getting all A's on my papers, even when I missed answers. Even when I missed them on purpose. There are lots of different ways of taking it out on people, like making them feel they don't even exist.

Mom and Jo

It's Mom and Jo's twelfth anniversary. They're going out to celebrate. Mom says Neenee and Poppa can't keep me overnight, so she asked our neighbor Jessica to come over and sit with me. I don't need a freakin' babysitter. Especially not *her*.

"Nick should be in bed by ten," Mom tells Jessica. "I left the number of the restaurant by the phone."

I roll my eyes at Jo. She doesn't see because she's gazing at Mom. She's lost in Mom. Mom is beautiful. She's dressed in a short black skirt with a sequined top and shawl. She has on high, spiky heels, and her long hair is coiled on top of her head.

Jo is wearing baggy black chinos and an ironed white shirt. Mom checks her watch. "We should go. The reservations are for seven."

"I'll tell you where I'd like to go," Jo whisper-purrs. She

spreads her hands on Mom's hips and twists her a little. Mom smiles, but steps out of Jo's embrace, glancing sideways at Jessica. Jessica looks bored. Or ugly. Because she is.

"Okay, off to Fairyland, Tinker Bell." Jo jangles her keys and wrenches open the front door. "Don't wait up," she says to me or Jessica or both of us. Her eyes brush Mom again and a faraway longing lodges in them. I long for them to leave so they can get back soon.

Mom bends down to kiss my cheek, but I lurch away. I don't want her slimy lipstick all over me.

When they're gone, the first thing Jessica does is check me out. I'm already staring at her. "What?" she says.

"Nothing," I mutter, and drop my eyes. She makes me sick. She's every eighth-grade girl, every girl who goes to the middle school, dressed in low-rider jeans with a canvas grommeted belt, a short shirt, and platforms.

When I leave for school and she's sitting on her stoop reading, sometimes she waves at me. I don't wave back. She's always with her friends, and whenever I pass, they huddle together and giggle. I know what they're laughing about.

"Give me a tour," she says.

"Of what?" I go. It's a house.

She gives me that stupid look.

"This is the living room." I point. "That's the kitchen."

She peers around the corner. Shouldering her beaded bag, she wanders into the kitchen. I think she'll head straight for the refrigerator, but she doesn't. She clomps toward the back. "What's in there?" she asks.

"You can't go in there."

Her eyes are fixed on the door. As if hypnotized, she's drawn to it.

"You're not allowed in there." I scurry to catch her. She's quick. "Don't go in." I lunge for her as she opens Mom and Jo's bedroom door.

"Stay out," I say. We have a rule. If the bedroom door is closed, privacy prevails. That goes for me and Mom and Jo. We respect each other's space. Jessica flips on the light and invades Mom and Jo's private space.

"Who sleeps here?" she asks, entering the room.

"None of your business."

She stalls halfway in, scoping out the area. It's cramped with the four-poster bed and the chest of drawers and the ironing board.

"Is this their room? Is this where they . . . do it?"

I click my tongue in disgust.

She swivels her head to look at me. "Have you ever seen them?"

"What do you mean?" I say. I see them every day.

Her head cocks at an odd angle. "You know. Have you seen them . . . have sex?"

"Shut up."

She twists back around and surveys the room again. What does she see? It's a normal bedroom. She spends a lot of time looking at the bed, scanning it. That's enough.

"Get out," I say. I hover on the threshold. I won't intrude.

Jessica opens her purse and pulls out a cell phone. She punches in a number and holds the cell to her ear. Turning slightly, she eyes me up and down. I hope she feels my fire. "You're not allowed in here," I repeat.

"Caitlin. Guess where I am." Jessica spins away and speaks into her cell. "I'm in their bedroom." She takes a step closer to the bed. "No, I'm not in the *bed*." The bed is unmade. The sheets and blanket are rumpled.

She reaches out and touches the bedpost. At the moment I decide to defy The Rule, she pivots and clunks in the other direction, toward the dresser. She studies the photos on top. Mom and Jo's wedding picture. My baby picture. A couple of strips of candid shots of the three of us taken at a photo booth in the mall.

"*How* much?" Jessica's eyes widen. "Would I have to get between the sheets?" She circles slowly back to the bed. "Oh my God, what if it makes me . . . " She glances over and catches my eye. "You know." Her face gets pink. She listens to her friend and giggles.

I charge across the floor and grab her arm. It's fat and mushy. I need both hands to get a grip. I yank her out of the room with more force than I know I have.

"Hey!" she cries. "Let go."

I slam Mom and Jo's bedroom door shut behind her. I impale myself against it, feet and arms spread apart. My chest is heaving and I'm shaking. I'm so angry I want to punch her.

"No," Jessica says under her breath. "The kid. Nick. He's . . . " She doesn't finish the sentence. She doesn't hang up either. In fact, the whole time she's here, she's on the phone. I crank up the TV in the living room full blast, but she doesn't care. She sprawls on the sofa with her shoes on and plays with her hair.

"Okay, I'll call later," I hear her say. In my peripheral vision, I see her sit up. I see her hesitate. "What's it like?"

I don't know why I turn and look. She's staring at me.

"What?" I say.

She has to raise her voice to be heard. "You know, having gay parents?"

I start to ignore her, but her expression is serious. I shrug. "It's okay. It's normal."

"Yeah, right," she goes.

"It is." To me.

"But . . . what do they do?" She leans forward.

I don't have to answer because her phone rings and she's back at it. Her voice changes when she's talking to her friends. She changes.

Ten o'clock comes and goes.

Ten forty-five.

At eleven fifteen, I start to worry. Where are Mom and Jo? They're never out this late. So far Jessica's called five people, and two have called her back. She has to know I can hear, even when she's speaking into her chest and muffling giggles. She's used the word "dyke" fifteen times.

She disgusts me. Everyone who says it disgusts me. I decide to wait for Mom and Jo in my room, where the company is better.

Lucky 2 lumbers in after me and jumps on my bed. One belly rub and she's out. Her snores lull me to sleep.

A sound wakes me suddenly. The front door. I jerk to attention. Mom and Jo are home.

I hear Jo ask, "How much do we owe you?"

As I roll out of bed and stagger toward the door, Jessica goes, "Thirty dollars."

"Holy crap," Jo says. "That's highway robbery."

Mom says, "Jo —"

Jessica's purse hits the floor. "Wait," she goes. "Uh, let me figure again."

"Here," Mom says. "Thank you for staying so late. Did Nick go to bed on time?"

"Uh, yeah," Jessica says, "I made sure."

She's such a liar. Mom better not give her a tip.

Jo says, "I'll walk you home."

Jessica yelps, "No! That's all right. I'll just run." She sounds scared of Jo. She should be. When I tell Mom and Jo what Jessica said . . . No, I won't tell. It happens all the time now, the slurs, the stares, the laughing behind our backs. I never tell.

The door closes, and I feel the house restore to normal. I climb back into bed, expecting Mom and Jo to tiptoe in for a night check. Minutes pass. I hear low music on the CD player and the floor creaking. I get up again to investigate.

My door is cracked and I peer through the narrow opening. The lights are off in the house. Mom and Jo are shoeless and they're dancing. They're dancing so close they're a single silhouette. Mom is caressing Jo's head to hers. They're cheek to cheek.

Jo says something, and Mom laughs. I think they've both been drinking. They kiss. The kiss goes on and on.

I don't need to see this.

I crawl back into bed and snuggle up against Lucky 2. Sure, Mom and Jo fight sometimes. They make up. That's what they do. It's times like this I know we'll always be together.

Who cares what people say? I love my moms.

Jo

September 21st. My eleventh birthday. Normally I'd be psyched, but a bunch of people from my new school are coming over for a party, and I'm dreading it. Jo made me invite them. I had no idea what she was planning until I woke up and checked out the backyard. Balloons and streamers. Party games. Pin the tail on the freakin' donkey, for chrissakes. I'm eleven, not seven.

I want to call everyone and tell them I have the flu, that I'm puking my guts out so they won't show up. It's too late. They start arriving.

I hardly know these people. After we moved to our new house in the city, it was tough starting over. Making friends; figuring out where I fit in. But everyone was pretty cool. A couple of the kids have lesbian moms, which is one reason we moved. So I wouldn't feel like such a freak. The other reason was because of this fight I got into with Josh Lever.

I guess I cracked a couple of his ribs. If the playground aide hadn't pulled me off him, I'd have crushed every bone in his body. He'd been calling me "queer" and "fag" all year, which was nothing new. Ever since kindergarten and "Dickless Nicholas,' I'd pretty much learned to live with the bashing. Calling my moms "dykes" and "homos" and "lesbos" was one thing, but Josh crossed the line when he said they were going to burn in hell.

Jo's right; sometimes you have to fight. The kickboxing lessons Jo and I took at the Y came in handy, as Josh found out. Ms. Gault told Jo and Mom that Josh's father was considering pressing charges. She advised us to switch schools.

Kerri and Reiko, Mom's friends from college, are here with their son, Takashi. He's in the other combined fifth-sixth class. Everyone calls him Taco. He's a jerk, but Kerri made my cake, so I had to invite him.

About an hour into it, everyone's laughing and having a good time. They're shouting out directions to the blindfolded person with the donkey tail, making them crash into the barbecue pit or trip over Lucky 2. I guess the party's going okay. It'd be better if Jo was here. As soon as Neenee showed up, Jo bailed.

Matt jabs me on the arm and says, "Can I try out your Muy Thais?"

"Sure," I tell him. I pull my new boxing gloves out of the box and hand them over. I'm glad Matthew came. I haven't seen him since the beginning of summer, and wouldn't have even recognized him if Jo hadn't razzed him about his bleached spikes and pierced earring. She said to me, "He's a pretty boy. A little faggy with the earring. Is he your new girlfriend?" I slugged her. Next to Matt I feel like a total geek, with my wire-rimmed glasses and shoulder-length hair.

A couple of the guys go over to watch Matt spar with my new training bag. It's a Typhoon — Jo's present to me. Mom got me the Kuhli loach and the Leopard Leaf fish I asked for. Neenee and Poppa bought me a laptop, which is cool, but I'll probably enjoy the fish and kickboxing equipment more. I told Jo that, but she still got mad. Where could she have gone? Neenee left right after I opened the presents. Jo could come back anytime now.

I see Mom and Kerri stacking the dirty plates from the picnic table and wander over to help. "Where could she be?" I ask Mom.

"Your guess is as good as mine," she replies evenly. Me, I'm mad. At first I was worried when Jo didn't get back in time for cake and ice cream. Now I'm pissed. She keeps doing this — taking off for hours at a time. Who knows where she goes?

I see Sasha McLaren, this girl in my class, sitting on the grass petting Lucky 2. Taco pops a balloon in her ear, and she shrieks. It spooks Lucky 2, who hobbles off toward the garage. Sasha looks at me and rolls her eyes. Really, I think. Taco's a turd.

The girls gather under the linden tree and start whispering about whatever it is they whisper about twelve hours a day. Sasha meets my eyes again and smiles. My face flares.

The guys all gravitate to the punching bag, and I'm wondering what to do now. I never had a boy-girl party. If Jo was here —

An explosion of sound splits the air. My ears squinch, it's so loud. Music. Mexican music. Mariachis. Trumpets blaring, like at Casa Consuelo, where we go for nachos. The back door screaks open, and Jo barrels into the yard. "Buenos dias, muchachos. Or is it, much nachos?" She cracks herself up. She's wearing a sombrero and carrying something under each arm. She pulls up, stomps twice in place, and announces, "Let the games begin."

One thing she's carrying is a donkey piñata, and she lugs it toward the linden tree. On her way past, she winks at me.

I shrink to disappear. Maybe if I stop breathing; stop living. Because I want to; I can smell it, the beer. She reeks. She's staggering across the yard like she's been guzzling for a week.

My eyes cut to Mom, who's frozen in her tracks with the carton of ice cream in her hand. A stream of chocolate sluices down her arm, but she doesn't notice. I notice. It's the only thing I'm concentrating on — that chocolate river of ice cream streaking toward Mom's elbow.

"Okay, who's firs'?" Jo asks.

I don't want to look. My eyes defy my brain. She's tied the piñata onto a branch of the tree, and now she's wielding the bat she'd tucked under her other arm. "Who's on firs'?" she says in a slur. "Wha's on secon'? I dunno's on third. 'Member that, Nicky?"

I meet Jo's eyes for the briefest moment and fire off a mental command: Don't. Don't do this to me.

"'Member?" she says louder.

The old Abbott and Costello routine we used to do when I was, like, four. I nod to shut her up.

"Batter, batterbatterbatter . . ." Jo swings the bat around in a circle, stumbling and nearly falling over. "Up."

Matt's voice enters the vacuum of my brain. "I'll go first." He hands me the boxing gloves and saunters across the yard toward Jo. Thank you, God, I pray to heaven.

Matt takes the bat and slings it over his shoulder. "Back up, everyone," he says. "I'm the state batting champ."

Which is a lie.

Jo stumbles back an inch, while everyone else moves forward to surround Matthew. He slices the air with the bat, and for a split second I will that bat to smack Jo right in the face.

I take it back.

She grins at me again, motioning me over.

The Mexican music that was drowning out my pulsing anger suddenly stops. Someone switched off the CD player inside. Mom?

"Nick!" Jo shouts.

"What?"

She sweeps an arm up and almost smacks her head.

My feet carry my spineless, boneless body across the lawn. Matt takes a wide arc at the piñata and misses. Everyone laughs. Jo especially. She's bent over, clutching her knees and wheezing with laughter. "Oh God. I'm going to pee my pants." She coughs.

"That was just a practice shot," Matt says. His eyes meet

mine, and I plead with him to kill that freakin' piñata; to pound it into dust and pulp and crepe paper confetti.

Matt hauls back and whacks the piñata. It doesn't break. The *whump* of the bat makes me wonder if the donkey is molded in cement or something. That'd be Jo's idea of a joke.

"You're out!" Jo thumbs over her shoulder. "Nex' batter."

Taco steps forward. "Give me that thing," he says.

"Nope." Jo stops him with a stiff-arm to his chest. "Girls' turn." She hitches her chin to the clot of girls. "C'mon. Sen' in your best jock."

Sasha looks at me, and I want to die.

Jo adds, "Oh Jesus H. Christ. Don't be so girly-girly."

My throat constricts. I won't cry. I feel my fists clench at my sides, and this raging urge to charge Jo, to ram her into the fence, is quelled when Sasha raises her hand and says, "I'll go."

"That's the spirit." Jo hands her the bat.

Sasha takes a good swing and whaps the piñata, but it doesn't break. She plants her feet. A fierce look of determination seizes her face.

"Whoo-ee," Jo calls through cupped hands. "Baa-ad girl."

Sasha smacks the piñata. Nothing. I'll rip that thing off the tree and throw it over the fence. . . .

"Good try." Jo tries to pat Sasha on the back as she passes, but misses and almost topples over. "Next up, the birthday boy."

Everyone turns to gawk at me. Only for a moment, though. Their eyes drop. A couple of the guys scrape their shoes through the grass.

"Haul ass, Nick. The candy in there's turning to donkey dung."

I storm over to Jo and wrench the bat out of her hands. Whirling, I club the piñata. Again. Again and again and again. I flail away, seeing red, hearing red. I batter and bruise that bloody donkey. On the upswing, the bat is jerked out of my hands.

"You're all such wusses," Jo says. She takes one swing, and the piñata cracks. Her next smack catches the branch and snags the jute holding up the piñata. It pulls loose, and the piñata rolls on the ground toward me. Before I can grab it, Jo lurches forward, trips, and sprawls on top of the donkey. It bursts apart.

All I hear is the snickering. And her laughing hysterically as she rolls over and goes, "Olé."

Nobody rushes in for the candy and prizes. I wish the ground would open up and swallow me. I don't hear Mom and Kerri approach from the rear. Mom claps once and says, "Okay, gang. Sorry to break up the party, but it's getting late." She loops an arm across my shoulders. "Thank everyone for coming, Nick."

Kerri smiles at me thinly. I don't smile back.

I wrench away from Mom and charge blindly for the house. Everything's fuzzy. Not only because I'm blinking back tears of rage. My glasses are gone. In the kitchen, I lift what's left of my birthday cake off the table and slam it against the wall.

✳

It's later. Nighttime. I vow never to emerge from my room. To rot in here until they have to ax down the door to get to my stinking, filthy, decomposing corpse. There's a knock, but I don't answer it. I've shoved my bureau against the door so no one can thwart my plan. Especially her.

No one tries.

Good.

The house is dead quiet. Almost. Our new house has two stories. Through the heater vent, I hear Mom upstairs in their bedroom, crying. I'd rather hear Jo yelling and know they're fighting. But they don't anymore. Jo just leaves.

My eleventh birthday, I think, staring vacantly at my vaulted bedroom ceiling. It's one for the memory book.

✳

There's a minor glitch in my plan to rot away. By morning I'm starving.

It's early when I wake up; scarcely dawn. My glasses aren't on my CD player, where I usually put them, so I dig out an old pair from my desk. As I pad through the living room, I notice a pillow and rumpled blanket on the sofa. I don't investigate. The last couple of months she's been sleeping there a lot. Instead, I make as much racket as possible tearing open a new carton of Pop-Tarts and inserting them into the toaster. Someone cleaned up the cake. Mom probably. I retrieve the canister of coffee out of the cupboard and brew a pot. That's when I see her through the kitchen window, in the backyard.

She's punching my Typhoon with her bare hands. Her knuckles are raw and scraped, and she's smearing blood all over the white vinyl. I watch her methodically beating my bag up. Beating herself up.

I can't stand it.

"Stop," I tell her, stepping between her and the bag. "Look what you're doing."

Jo gazes down at her hands as if they're not even attached to her body. She lowers them. She says, "I've got a problem."

"No shit," I reply.

Her head lolls back and I can see she's hurting. "I made you coffee," I tell her, thumbing at the mug on the picnic table. "Extra strong."

She asks, "Did you spike it with arsenic?"

"We're all out," I answer. "Unfortunately, all I could find was Excedrin."

She drags over to the table, and I wrap my arms around the punching bag for a moment, willing myself to be strong. I want to hate her, but I can't. Not because the emotion isn't there. It's just . . . this is Jo.

As I slide in across from her, she says in a raspy voice, "I'm sorry, Nick."

I don't meet her eyes. "This has to be the last time," I tell her. "Mom and I can't take this anymore."

Her fingers, threaded around the coffee mug, tighten at the joints. "My parents are both falling-down drunks. Did I ever tell you that?"

I meet her eyes now. I wondered why, whenever my

"other" grandparents were mentioned, she'd always change the subject. "Where are they?" I ask.

"I don't know. I took off when I was sixteen. Never looked back."

She looks . . . beaten.

"It's no excuse," I inform her.

"I know." She buries her face in her mug.

I add, "Kids don't have to be stupid like their parents. You're the one who told me that."

"When?" She blinks up.

I don't remember. It's something Jo would say.

The silence between us builds, the way it's been doing. I hate it. She sips her coffee and sets the mug down. "It's over, Nick," she says. Her eyes lock on mine. "I quit. I promise I'll never take another drink as long as I live."

Sure, I think.

She holds my eyes. Hers are steady, serious.

She extends her fist for me to knuckle knock. It's bloody, so I hesitate.

Or maybe I hesitate because I'm wondering if this is the real Jo, the one who's as good as her word. Or the other Jo, the one who's good for nothing, as Mom said last time she got home and found Jo passed out again. I remember something Jo said to me once about Santa Claus. Matthew told me Santa Claus was a hoax, that our Christmas presents were really left under the tree by our parents. I didn't want to believe that. I didn't want to think that what I'd believed in so long and so hard wasn't true. Jo said, "Nick, nobody can tell you what to believe in. As long as you feel deep down in your heart that something's true, then it is. For you."

Deep down in my heart I want to believe in the real Jo. I want to believe she's back, as good as ever.

I ball a fist. My knuckles rap hers lightly, so it won't hurt. "I'll help you quit," I say.

"Good." She cricks a lip. "I'm going to need it." Sniffling, she wipes her nose on her sleeve and adds, "Shit. I have to quit my job. Your mom's going to kill me."

We both laugh at this. Jo just got this new job a week ago — tending bar at The Sports Grille.

I say, "I hear Denny's is hiring."

Jo reaches over and smacks me upside the head. She pauses and runs her palm down the side of my face.

I feel my throat catch, and I slide out the end of the bench. "My Pop-Tarts are burning," I say.

Jo calls, "Wait a minute. I've got a present for you." She fishes in her hip pocket and yanks out my glasses; she tosses them to me. "I wouldn't want you stumbling through life the way I do," she says. "You might step in donkey doo."

✳

I don't have a memento of that day. Nothing in my scrapbook. There's only her promise and a blank page where my eleventh birthday oughta be.

Jo

"It's kid's night," Jo tells Mom. "Something new they're trying out at AA."

Mom looks at Jo. I know she's not buying it, but she lets me go. As we're climbing into Beatrice, Jo pauses and says, "Hold on. I forgot the gun."

I flinch. "What?"

She fumbles in the garage through her mess of tools and scrap wood and car parts and returns with my paintball marker.

"Why do we need that?"

Jo slides the gun behind her seat and revs the engine. "It's part of my twelve-step program." She shifts into reverse. "Step one: Step on it."

I don't ask. This is Jo.

She cranks up the radio to earsplitting volume, which I love. We're tuned to 105 FM, our favorite station. Hot

LED. The hard-core rock fissures your bones and fries your brain.

We're deaf as rocks when we pull into the parking lot at Tony's Liquors.

I narrow my eyes at Jo.

"Wait here," she says, flinging open the door and launching out. I watch her open the grated door and disappear inside. A slow burn ignites in my core and spreads up to my chest, through my head, to my ringing ears. She promised. *Promised*.

A minute later she hops back in, toting two twelve-packs and another paper bag, all of which she shoves behind us in the cab.

I'm seething. I'm fuming. The fire from my eyes scabs the plastic on the dash. She says, "Anyone ever tell you you look exactly like your mother when she's pissed off?"

I fold my arms and twist my torso to glare out the window.

Jo sighs. "And you're just about as trusting."

We spew gravel as we peal out. Usually, we holler over the pounding bass to talk, joke around, hurl insults, but we're not speaking this trip. At least I'm not. Jo heads out to the country.

We drive for about twenty minutes, beyond the city, the last housing development, and turn onto a dirt road. A NO TRESPASSING sign whizzes by. Jo veers Beatrice directly into the woods and rumbles through the trees. I hang on to my seat as my teeth chatter. We crunch to a stop at the end of the road, and the music cuts out. "Grab the flashlight," Jo says.

I sit for a minute, brooding. She promised. *Promised*.

"Nick! What'd I say?" she yells from outside. Her door slams.

It's pitch black. I grab the Coleman lantern, the only flashlight I can find. I don't see Jo, and panic.

"Over here," she calls.

My heart's racing. What are we doing? It's eerie. There's no one here. Animal eyes are watching us, though. I can sense them observing our every move, tasting dinner.

"This is a good place. Set her up."

What does she mean? "Set what up?"

Jo rips into a twelve-pack and lifts out two beers, one in each hand. With her teeth she pops the tops. Tipping the cans, she drains them onto the ground. The beer fizzes and foams at her feet. She sets the emptied cans on an old log behind her and stacks. Four in a row. Three between the four. Two on top. One at the peak. "Give us some light," she orders.

There's a thick crescent moon, but it's gauzy, like a ghost story. I flick on the lantern and flash the head beams over Jo's handiwork. She's building another pyramid on a rock formation to her right, and I notice in the light there are dozens of cans littered around the area. Maybe hundreds. So this is where she comes.

"Nick, what the hell are you doing? Pick a spot and hang the lamp. Let's get this show on the road."

If I poke the nearest limb through the handle, the beams shine in the wrong direction, toward Beatrice, where Jo's headed. Where's she going? I decide to wedge the lantern between two branches of a skinny pine tree. It illuminates all the cans, like a helicopter strobe spotlighting debris from a plane crash.

Jo guns the engine and I freak. Is she leaving me here? I sprint back, tripping over a root and taking a header. My glasses fly.

I grope around.

"For my next kid, I'm requesting the coordination gene," Jo says. I get up and brush the pine needles off my hands and knees. My glasses dangle from Jo's pinkie finger, and I snatch them off. "What the hell are we doing out here?" I snarl.

She slugs me on the arm. Hoisting herself onto the truck bed, she extends a hand to me. While I was sucking dirt, she'd backed Beatrice around.

I don't need help. She's got two of our plastic lawn chairs in the truck bed, scootched up close to the cab. As she plops in the left one, she motions me down to the right. I sit. She hands me the marker. Goggles land in my lap. "Still remember how to use this baby?"

"Duh," I say. Granted, the marker didn't get a lot of use. When Jo bought it for me last Christmas, Mom had a cow. She told Jo to return it. Jo refused. "You know I hate guns," Mom said. "We'll be careful," Jo countered. Mom actually shouted, "No! Take it back. I forbid guns in this house."

Jo said, "I'm not taking it back."

Mom stormed to her room.

Jo could take it back if they were going to fight about it. I didn't care. Except . . . I did. I really wanted a paintgun. Matt had a semiauto Spyder. He played paintball with his dad almost every weekend.

The only time I ever got to shoot was when Jo and I snuck out. We'd tell Mom we were going to a hockey game or something and drive to the firing range. Mostly we'd target shoot. This one time we went to a real field where a tournament was being held — guys in camo flanking bunkers and snapshooting. It looked like a blast. Jo and I were dying to get out there.

We hadn't gone to shoot paintball in a while. Not since Jo joined AA.

"What am I shooting at?" I ask, sighting through my goggles an eternal forest of black.

"Duh," Jo mocks. "The cans?"

Our voices muffle in our masks. Is this what she does? All those nights she's supposed to be at AA? I lower the gun. "You promised," I say accusingly.

Jo tilts her head. She looks like an alien, like Darth Vader. "I promised I'd quit drinking. I didn't say how." She lifts the barrel in front of my face. "Shoot."

"You told Mom —"

"I told her I'd join AA. I did. Are you going to shoot or not?"

I lodge the CO_2 tank against my armpit. She's loaded

yellow balls. I sight a can and squeeze the trigger, then realize I forgot to cock for the first shot. Jo doesn't say what I'm thinking: Shit for brains.

Finally I get off a shot and miss. "We're too far away," I say.

Jo takes the marker. She fires. Splat. The top can on the log pyramid sails backward and bounces off a tree. Jo licks her finger and air marks a score. She hands me the gun.

"Did you ever go?" I ask. Because I'm curious. To what depths will Jo sink to deceive Mom? Or me.

"To an AA meeting? Yeah, I went. Once." Jo pushes her goggle mask up onto her head. "It brought back memories. Bad ones."

I raise the marker. "Like what?" I take aim.

"Like Alateen, which I did a few times when I was growing up. It didn't take. I hate that group shit. The whole touchy-feely thing reminds me of church. Let's hug and pray and ask forgiveness from Our Heavenly Father as we poor wretched souls cling to each other in this hour of need, this time of desperation." Jo wiggles her hands in the air. "Hallelujah."

I crack a smile. But I'm listening.

"Where was my Heavenly Father when my heavenly mother was puking up all over the bathroom floor? When I'd get up in the middle of the night and slip in that shit? I'd get it all over me and have to clean it up. Where was He — where was anyone — on the nights my folks even bothered to come home at all? Where was Alateen then?" Jo levels the barrel. "Are you going to shoot or what?"

I squeeze the trigger. Whoosh. The paintball zings into the trees. I wasn't really aiming.

Jo yanks her goggles back down over her face. "Come on, sissy miss," she muffles. "You can do it. If I can do it, you can do it."

I squint and line up the label on the Budweiser can directly in the center of the gun barrel. *Pop. Splat.* A can pitches to the left. Yeah! I punch the air.

"We're even," Jo says in a fuzzy voice. She reaches for the marker, but I don't relinquish it.

"What?"

I slide up my goggles. So does she. I ask her point-blank. "Are you still drinking?"

Jo holds my eyes. Her head starts to wobble and bob. "You know, Nick," she goes. Broken neck. "I got my own twelve-step program. Steps number one through eleven" — her eyeballs bounce around — "do what you need to do to get it done. Step number twelve: Never drink alone." She gets up and hurdles the side of the truck, crunching to a landing. From the cab, she retrieves the paper bag. She slings it over the side and, stepping on the rusted wheel hub, levers herself up and over. From the bag, she removes a plastic bottle and unscrews the lid. The contents hiss. She hands it to me and opens one for herself.

"Cheers queers." She chucks her bottle on mine.

It's Coke. We slug it back in unison. She hasn't answered my question, but I don't press. She promised, and I have to trust she's as good as her word. This is Jo. I want to believe.

*

Here's what I believe today: Until you're old enough to see your parents for who they really are, you can't trust a word they tell you. I don't ask, and Jo doesn't tell. If she's not drinking again after everything that's happened, I can't imagine what would make her start.

Mom and Jo

We've lined up our chaises on the patio deck facing directly into the sun. It's a hundred degrees, easy, but beach bums don't care. Today is the last day of summer. Tomorrow I start seventh grade. I'm not obsessing about that — yet. I'm thinking about whether I should smear more sunscreen on my nose so it won't peel again. We've slathered every other inch of exposed skin around our swimsuits and put on our matching shades. Now we're just hanging out, catching some rays. Suckin' up the shit-end of summer, as Jo says.

"Turn it up," I call across to her. "What's the score?"

Jo reaches down to amp up the volume on the radio she's set between her and Mom. "Still goose eggs," she answers. "Top of the sixth." She retrieves the bottle of sunscreen and squeezes a blob onto Mom's stomach.

Mom yelps and drops her paperback to the side of her chaise. Jo rubs in the lotion and I watch, behind my shades.

I follow the slow circles over Mom's stomach, around her belly button — the way Mom's skin shimmers in the sun. I wonder what it'd feel like to rub suntan lotion on Sasha McLaren's bare skin. The thought makes me hot, and not from the sun. I close my eyes and dream.

"Hey, Nick. Would you run in and get me a water?" Mom tickles my leg with her big toe.

"What am I, your slave?"

Mom and Jo answer in unison, "Yes." Jo adds, "While you're at it, bring me a cold wet one."

I lower my shades to eye her. She sneers at me.

I hear them whispering behind my back as I fling open the screen door. They laugh. I don't even care if they're laughing about me. They're laughing more, like they used to. It's better since Jo quit drinking.

In the refrigerator I spy the watermelon I picked out at the farmer's market this morning. Perfectly round, perfectly ripe. It makes me hungry. I slice it into wedges and stack them in a Tupperware bowl. I balance two Cokes and a bottle of water on top.

Sneaking up behind Mom, I roll her water bottle across her greasy stomach, and she squeals. Jo snorts and slaps my hand.

Mom tips her shades. "Ooh, watermelon." She smiles up at me. "Good idea, Nick." Scooting to sit up, she adds, "By the way, what are you making for dinner?"

I pop the top on my Coke. "I thought I'd barbecue burgers and brats. I made celery cream cheese with bacon bits, and strawberry shortcake for dessert."

Jo says, "Will you listen to him? Celery cream cheese and strawberry sorbet." She flaps a limp wrist at me. "How gay."

I bristle, but let it pass. "Shortcake," I repeat under my breath. I don't know why the whole gay thing has started to bother me lately. Everyone says it to everyone. "You're so gay. How gay." They don't mean anything.

But seventh grade . . . Two moms . . .

Mom kicks Jo. "Don't knock it. Kerri says Nick's a born chef." Mom reaches over and trails her fingers through my long hair. Last month she talked me into taking this cooking class from Kerri. It was all right, even if I was the only guy. Someone's got to cook around here. Mom adds, "We should've bought more of these from the slave traders. One to clean the house. One to mow the lawn. . . ."

"One to kiss my ass." Jo whaps me.

For some reason, that triggers a question I've been meaning to ask for a long time. "Do you know who my father is?" I know I have to have one.

Mom and Jo exchange a look. A staggering silence closes in around us, and I think I'm sorry I brought it up. Jo clears her throat and says, "Uh, yeah. He's a syringe full of sperm."

Mom clicks her tongue. She takes a glug of water and says, not looking at me, "Have you been wondering about that?"

Jo says before I do, "Duh." She widens her eyes at me like, Of course he's been wondering about it. I also catch the vibe from her that we should discuss it later, in private.

The thing is, I want to talk about it now with both of them here. "Who is he?" I ask. "Do you know? Did you meet him?" And the real question: "Can I meet him?"

Mom snaps, "No."

I snap back, "Why not?"

Jo says, "Okay, we weren't going to tell you this, but we promised to always be truthful with you. Your father is a six-hundred pound Buddhist monk with a hunchback and a harelip."

Mom blows water out her nose. She coughs and splutters.

Jo adds, "And you look just like him."

I pitch Mom's book at Jo. I'm grinning, though; I can't help it. "Really, can I find out who he is?" I ask Mom.

She daubs at her watery eyes. "I don't think so, honey. The sperm donation centers have strict confidentiality rules."

I knew about the sperm bank. Jo explained that part to me. But they have to have a record of who . . . deposited.

Jo says, "Think about it. Would you want to get up one morning and find a hundred kids at your door all holding out their arms crying, 'Daddy, Daddy.'"

I just look at her.

"Well? Would you?"

I lie back in my chaise and let the image swirl around in my head. Okay, Jo has a point. Even if I did find out who he was, he'd be a total stranger. He wouldn't be my father. He might be rich and famous, though. A celebrity or a sports figure. With me as a kid? Right. More likely, he'd be a geek. Or worse — a drug addict. I mean, what kind of guy sells his juice, anyway?

Something prickles my chest, and a black seed slides down into my lap. I blink up and catch another one smack in the eye.

"Bull's-eye." Jo laughs.

I chomp a bite of watermelon and load up on ammunition.

"Hold it." Mom covers her head. She leans forward so Jo and I have unobstructed battle lines.

Jo's fast, but her aim sucks. I'm good at this. It requires more luck and speed than skill or vision. I shoot all the seeds in one wedge of watermelon, then grab another. Meanwhile, Mom's at the edge of her chaise spitting seeds out into the yard for Savage to pounce on. It's pretty funny. Jo and I call a truce to watch. Eventually we join Mom.

Savage gets bombarded. After a while he tires of the abuse and wanders off to stalk a grasshopper. "Let's have a seed-spitting contest," Mom says.

"You're on." Jo spits a seed at Mom.

"Not at each other." Mom flicks the seed off her arm. "We'll go for distance."

"Okay." I spit-fire three seeds that all land on my foot. Jo howls.

"Shut up." Between my index finger and thumb, I pinch a seed. It strikes Jo in the chest and slides down her cleavage into her swimsuit. I giggle. "Booby prize."

Jo says, "Yeah, you're a real crack shot." She digs out the seed and threatens me with it.

"Wait." Mom holds up a hand. "We need to establish official rules."

Jo and I groan in unison. "We never should have let her to go to law school," Jo mutters.

"Really," I agree.

Mom ignores us. "We each get three tries to shoot as far as possible. We'll mark our farthest seed —"

"Hold on." I push to my feet. "I have a better idea. Let's shoot for accuracy."

"We never should have let him out of reform school," Jo mutters. She slides her shades up over her head.

I stack the watermelon wedges on the picnic table behind us and cart the empty Tupperware bowl out across the long grass. Halfway to the linden tree, I position the bowl on the ground. I eyeball whether it's equidistant from each of us. Looks good.

Jo cocks her head. "Should we devise a point system, like yard darts?"

Returning, I say what Jo always does: "That'd be anal retentive." She yanks on my leg hairs and I swat at her hand.

Mom says, "Okay, we can spit as many seeds as we can hold in our mouths. We'll go in rounds. Whoever gets the most seeds in the bowl wins."

"Wins what?" I ask, perching on the edge of my chaise.

We think on this. Jo decides, "A trip to the Bahamas, all expenses paid. In your case, Nick, a one-way ticket."

I shove her head. She twists my wrist.

Mom adds, "Or you can choose the car/boat package, unless you'd rather have the cash."

"We'll take the cash," Jo and I say together.

The three of us seal the deal with a unified knuckle knock.

Mom lifts a wedge of watermelon off the stack and hands it to Jo. Mom takes a wedge and I take one. Jo leans over and says directly in my ear, "May the bad seed win."

"You wish."

Mom removes her shades and sets them on the ground. Her eyes gleam. Her jaw sets. She doesn't have to say it: This is war. I remember now why Jo and I refuse to play board games with her.

As if on cue we all start gobbling watermelon. I'm concentrating so hard on separating seeds and storing artillery in my cheek that I don't notice what my opponents are doing. I toss the rind away. Glancing over, I see Mom and Jo poised and ready to shoot. We all have our game faces on.

At that moment Lucky 2 scrabbles out from under the picnic table. She lumbers around in front of us and swishes her tail. I catch it first — the stench that'd knock a skunk unconscious. I can't help it; I cough and lose my seeds. The trail of noxious fumes reaches Mom and Jo at the same time and they both choke. Seeds and watermelon juice dribble from our mouths and drip down our fronts and we look at one another and crack up. We laugh so hard we double over. Hysterical, we collapse our chaises. Then Jo attacks Mom. She gathers up a handful of seeds off the grass and starts chasing her, sticking them down her bikini bottoms and wrestling her to the grass. When I get in on the action, Mom screams.

As we're pinching seeds into each other's hair and sticking them down our swimsuits, I'm thinking, This is it. My Defining Moment. That's what Jo calls it. The one memory that stays freshest in your mind and marks a turning point. The moment in time that characterizes what your life will be about.

*

Stupid. A seed-spitting contest? It was a small, insignificant moment. Except . . . it wasn't. Later that night, I remember, I got up, went outside, and crawled around on my hands and knees to comb through the grass for a seed. One seed for my scrapbook. Talk about crazy.

Talk about premonition.

I mean, how could I know? How could I know then that a watermelon seed would symbolize the last summer we'd ever have together?

Jo

I'm stoked. Sasha McLaren asked me out today. At least, I think she did. The invitation to this dance at her church was relayed through her friend Alexis to my friend Zeke to me while a bunch of us guys played Horse at the hoops after lunch. It went: "If Sasha asked you" — dribble, dribble — "to this dance at her church" — aim, layup — "would you, like, go?" Shoot, score an H. My answer: "Well . . . yeah." Rebound, dribble. "If she asked." Shoot. Miss.

I figure that's as close to a personal invitation from a girl as I'm ever going to get.

The dance is this Saturday night. Two days away. I think, If she doesn't call me tonight, I'll call her. I've known Sasha's phone number since we worked on Odyssey of the Mind together. Sometimes I punch in the numbers, wait for the phone to ring, and hang up. To practice, just in case.

In case I work up an odyssey of courage.

I'm flying high when I hit the front door at home. On the way, I decided I won't wait until tonight. I'll call her now. Confirm. Ask her what time; where's it at; should I pick her up. Details. Start planning. Ask Jo what I should wear. How to act. She'll razz me, but that's the price for being a stud. The door is already open, which is weird. Usually I'm the first one home.

Then I see her. Jo. She's hunched over on the edge of the sofa, elbows on her knees, chin pressed between her palms. "Nicky," she says, lifting her head. "Hey."

She never calls me Nicky. The look on her face, her . . . voice. It's bad. "Is it . . . ?" My throat constricts. I let the question dangle because I don't want to know the answer.

Jo frowns. She understands instantly and shakes her head. "No. No, it isn't Lucky. She's fine."

I exhale relief. Lucky 2 had had a hard time breathing over the weekend. We rushed her to the vet, and he diagnosed heart disease. He said there wasn't much he could do and gave us some pills. "It's only a matter of time," he told us. Which could mean a day, a month, a year. I prayed for a year.

As if on cue, Lucky 2 straggles in from the kitchen and chuffs at me. The way she does to welcome me home. I crouch down to give her a hug. I'm not ashamed to admit I love this dog. I love Savage and my fish too, but there's something about losing Lucky 2 that makes me afraid, makes me panic, like I'll be losing something bigger when she's gone.

But she's fine. She's here. Breathing better. I feel totally relieved until Jo says, "Sit down, Nick. We need to talk."

"Just a sec," I tell her. "I'm dying of thirst." I'm not really, but Jo's tone of voice makes my heart race. I fling open the fridge and study the contents. There's the chicken I pulled from the freezer this morning to thaw. I'll need to get it dressed and in the oven pretty soon. I'm making Stove Top stuffing. Or I could boil the chicken; make a stew. Mom loves my fricasseed chicken and dumplings.

"Nick? What the hell are you doing?"

Stalling. We're out of soda, so I snag a Sunny D for me and one for Jo. On the way back to the living room, I notice it. The silence. No music. Jo hasn't even turned on the TV for background noise. Now I'm really afraid.

"Thanks," she says, taking the bottle of juice from me. She doesn't open it. She sets it on the end table and stares at it, as if she's never seen a Sunny D before.

"You won't believe what happened today," I say, flopping into the armchair across from her. "You remember Sasha McLaren? From OM? She asked me out." After Jo hassles me, she'll tell Mom. Mom'll be like, "Where does she live? Do we know her parents?" Jo'll go, "What are your intentions, young man?" Like I'm going to marry her or something. Jo'll say, "Do we need to pay a visit to the birds and the bees?" This is where it'll get embarrassing, when it'll meander into condom territory.

"I don't want to talk about that right now," Jo says. "Listen — your mom has cancer." She meets my eyes and holds them.

What? I don't hear her. Yes I do, but I continue, "She invited me to this dance, or at least I think she did, or she's going to, or —"

"Breast cancer." Jo picks up her juice. Her hand is shaking. She sets the bottle down again. "It's bad, Nick."

My heart seizes. There's this roar in my ears like a battalion of tanks rumbling through with an army of marching marines. Jo gets up and crosses the room. She squeezes beside me in the armchair. Snaking an arm behind my neck, she cups my ear in her hand and pulls me to her chest.

I say, barely breathing, "Is she going to die?"

Jo's heart is hammering, and I hear her inhale a raspy breath. "That's a possibility."

"No." Tears spring to my eyes. "Please. Promise me she won't die."

Jo's arm tightens around me. Then both arms. "I can't do that. I wish I could, Nicky. God, how I wish I could."

I know I shouldn't, but I start bawling. Jo holds me. She explains how Mom needs an operation. Surgery. A mastectomy. How they're going to cut off her left breast.

I try to picture this, but I can't. I don't want to.

Words clog my brain. Questions. After the surgery, Jo says, Mom will probably undergo radiation, maybe even chemo. "She might be fine, Nick. The surgery and radiation might take care of it. They don't know. They just don't know. She didn't go to the doctor right away when she found the lump, so it's pretty advanced. But that doesn't mean she won't pull through."

I clutch Jo's arm. I swipe my nose on her sleeve.

"She's a fighter."

No, I think. She's not.

Jo jostles me a little. "Hey, we have to be strong for her,

okay? It's our job to keep her happy. Keep her spirits up." She pushes me away to gaze into my eyes. "Got that?" Jo grips my shoulders, hard. "None of this weepy, dopey don't-die-on-me shit. She doesn't need that. None of us do."

I nod. I'm not sure I can be that strong, but I promise I'll try. I'll try. I have this sudden urge, this need to tell Mom about my day. Tell her about Sasha, how she asked me out. How she's tall and pretty and popular too. How she likes me. Me. Nicholas Nathaniel Thomas Tyler. I want to share my happiness with Mom. "Where is she?" I ask Jo.

Jo eases me off her and pushes to her feet. She crosses over to the bookshelf and, reaching up, runs a finger vertically down our last family photo. A dust track splits the picture in half. It's the one we shot last spring out back with Lucky 2 and Savage. Jo says, "She went to tell her family. She asked me to tell you. She just —" Jo stops and swallows hard. "She couldn't." She exhales a shallow breath. "Her surgery is Monday morning, Nick. If you want to ditch tomorrow, you're allowed." Jo turns and forces a smile. "I am."

I think, I'll never go back to school. I'm never leaving this house. I'll never, ever let either of them out of my sight again.

Mom

I'm waiting for her when she drives up. She doesn't get out of the car right away because she's talking on her cell. She rests her head against the steering wheel, phone pressed to her ear. I rise from the stoop and hustle down the front walk. When I tap on the glass, she jerks her head up and blinks fast. She blinks away tears. She says something into the phone and folds it closed.

Mom opens the door. "That was Kerri. She wants to know if you're interested in this gourmet cooking class she's teaching —"

I throw my arms around Mom's middle. Then I pull back immediately in case I hit her too hard. Hit her . . . breast.

She lifts my hair over my right shoulder and smiles down on me. Somber smile. Sobering smile. "Jo told you."

I nod. I try, try not to disintegrate into tears.

"It's going to be fine," Mom says. She presses her hands gently to my ears and rests her chin on my head.

"What did you find? I mean, Jo said a lump. What kind of lump?" What does it feel like? I want to ask. Where is it? How big a lump? Couldn't she see it? When did it appear?

Mom sighs. I know that sigh. "I don't want to talk about that. Not with you, honey."

Why? I want to scream. Why can't you tell *me*?

She shoulders her bag and I take her hand. Her hand is smaller than mine now. I shrink in size, in time. I'm suddenly four and holding her hand at Thanksgiving, feeling safe and secure. But not whole. Not without Jo.

Without Mom . . . ?

The possibility is unimaginable.

"What's for dinner?" Mom asks as we walk to the house.

I can't speak. I can only look at her and see her. Memorize her. Burn her into my brain and vow to never let go of her.

Mom says, "Nick, you're hurting my hand."

I loosen my grip, but not entirely. "Chicken nuggets," I say. "We're having chicken nuggets and creamed corn." I changed my mind about the fricassee.

Mom wrinkles her nose. She doesn't remember about making me chicken nuggets and creamed corn that night. Her eyes drift to the door, and what she sees alters her expression. I don't recognize the look. Dread? Sorrow? As if crossing the threshold and entering this house will signify everlasting doom. That can't be it. Jo's inside, standing at the door, meeting Mom's eyes, and searching.

Mom squeezes my hand and releases me. Or tries to. "I

don't think we can both fit through the door, Nick. You're going to have to let go."

I don't want to. But I do because she asks. I vow to do anything she asks for the rest of my life.

✳

She ran a bath that night, I remember, after dinner. The TV blared in the living room and the phone rang. No one bothered to get it. I lay in bed with Lucky 2's head on my chest, stroking her fur. Her warmth and the bulk of her body felt sure and solid. I listened, waited for the change. There was one coming, I knew. It wasn't a sound that would register in the range of human hearing. More a feeling. A tremor at first, then moving, shaking. Underneath me, the house quaked and cracked, as if the foundation was crumbling. I held on to Lucky 2 for life.

Then Jo stuck her head in to check on me like she did every night. I squeezed my eyes shut, feigning sleep. The earthquake subsided.

I waited for Mom to come in and kiss me goodnight. But she didn't.

When the tears came, I couldn't stop them. For the first time in my life, I cried myself to sleep.

Jo

I'm up early to fix breakfast. My eyes are swollen and they burn. I don't care. I have to cook. I want to make something special for Mom. She didn't eat last night when she came home from Neenee and Poppa's. She said she wasn't hungry; she had a headache. All she wanted to do was run a bath and go to bed.

I brew a pot of coffee. There's not much food in the house, and as I'm thinking about calling Kerri to ask how to make a soufflé, Mom rushes out, dressed, shoving books and papers into her carryall. She says, "You're going to be late, Nick. You're not even dressed."

Jo's behind Mom on the stairs.

My eyes meet Jo's. She says, "I gave Nick the day off."

Mom whirls. "Why?"

Jo widens her eyes at Mom. Which isn't easy for her in

the morning. She's usually bleary-eyed and half-alive. To-day I know how she feels.

Mom digs in her purse for her cell and checks to see if there are messages on her voice mail. She punches in a se-ries of numbers. "No." She holds the phone to her ear. "You have to go to school."

"Erin, come on."

"No." Mom listens a minute and folds her phone closed. She rushes past us, past Jo who's now at the bottom of the stairs. "I don't have time to argue. I have a test today and a paper due on Monday. Shit." Mom conks her forehead with the phone. "I'll have to send it in."

"Erin!" Jo says. "For God's sake." She chases down Mom to the door.

"No," I hear Mom bark. "Nothing's changed. Don't treat me like an invalid, Jo. Nick," she orders in a voice that car-ries across the abyss, "go to school."

The storm door shuts. Jo hollers, "At least sit down with us and eat breakfast."

A minute later the car starts.

Jo returns, shaking her head at me. She flops into her chair at the kitchen table and rakes her hands through her tangled hair. "That woman will be the death of me," she murmurs.

I stop breathing. Jo jerks up and swivels her head around. "Nick, God. I'm sorry. It's just an expression. I didn't mean —"

I'm mad suddenly. Furious. I yank out the plug on the coffee pot and storm to my room. Before I can slam the door,

Jo's wedged her body between it and me. "People handle fear in different ways. Pain too. You know that." Her eyes fix on my face. "I know you know."

My stomach grinds. I force it down – the anger, ache, the need.

"Want to go shooting?" Jo asks. "Mark a few cans? Or hang out at the Y and spar? We should go somewhere, work it off."

I shake my head. If you ignore the problem, it'll go away. That's Mom's philosophy of life. It isn't working so great for her, but I figure I'll give it a shot. "I'm going to school," I say.

Jo's head bobs. "You're going to school. Great." She smacks the door. "Lay a guilt trip on me. Now I have to go to work. Thanks a lot."

She leaves, but a minute later she's back. "Nick. You know I'm here for you, right? You know you can talk to me."

I'm pulling a T-shirt over my head and don't have to answer.

"Nick!"

"Yeah!"

"Okay. All right." She sniffs. "I didn't want you to worry about that. You don't ever need to worry about that."

Mom

"What is this?" Mom examines the plastic Jell-O cup. "Come over here, Nick, and tell me if this looks edible to you."

Jo and I both peer down at Mom's tray, at the package of Saltines and cup of lime Jell-O. I think it's lime. It's opaque, green, and watery. I almost say, "It looks like your Thanksgiving Jell-O without the mini marshmallows," but Jo pipes up, "If the cancer doesn't kill you, the food here will."

Mom tries to smile. It comes out a wince. She's still a little woozy from the surgery, and obviously sore. She hasn't moved her left arm since they brought her back from recovery. Since they let us up to the room. My eyes keep straying there; staring at the place where they cut off her breast. I want to see. It's morbid, I know, but I want to see the hole.

Jo reaches into the back pocket of her jeans and pulls out

her wallet. "Here, Nick." She slips me a twenty. "Go across the street to that BK and buy us each a Whopper."

"I'm not really hungry," Mom says. "Why don't you two go? You've been here all day. Why don't you go home and go to bed?"

"Okay." Jo slings a leg over the railing on Mom's bed like she's climbing in with her. I consider circling around to the other side, but that's her left side. The one with the hole.

Mom says wearily, "Not now, Jo." She shuts her eyes. Jo stumbles getting out. She runs her knuckles across Mom's cheek and smoothes her hair. "You should eat, hon. There's broth or something in this bowl. Try that."

"I can't," Mom says. "I'm sick."

A nurse comes in to check on Mom, so Jo and I fade into the background. There's a leather chair in the corner, where I've tossed my backpack, and a short sofa where Jo's spread out the newspaper. I open my pack to retrieve my Game Boy. I don't know why I brought it. Mom got it for me at Wal-Mart one time when I went shopping with her. This other kid was throwing a temper tantrum in the aisle and Mom said, "I'm so glad you're mine." I didn't even ask for it and she bought me a Game Boy.

As the nurse takes Mom's blood pressure, she remarks, "I understand you're going to law school."

Jo pipes up, "She's graduating in the spring."

"Maybe," Mom murmurs.

"You are," Jo counters. "You have to. We already bought your present." Jo winks at me. We haven't bought it yet, but we picked it out. Jo says to the nurse, "She has a job lined up at this swanky law firm in the burbs. What is it again, Nick? Johnson and Johnson? Abbott and Costello?"

"Heckel and Jeckel," I say. It's a running joke. We started running it on the way to the hospital. "Bonnie and Clyde."

The nurse chuckles and peeks under Mom's gown. Mom's eye catches mine. She looks away. The lump in my throat swells, and as hard as I try I can't swallow it down. I can't stop looking at her, either. I have to remember how she looks. How she looked, yesterday. The day before, when she was whole. Already I'm having trouble remembering.

I should've saved something. A picture. A drawing. The images in my mind are blurring and fading.

At the moment Mom looks terrible. Her hair is plastered to her head and her eyes are sunken. Her skin is gray. What if this is my last memory of her? I see a black, bloody hole. The horrid vision evaporates, but the fear doesn't. Or the odor. It's not only the hospital smell, it's Mom's smell. Like cancer. Like death.

The nurse asks if Mom's in any pain and she says no. She's lying.

There's a rap at the door, and a familiar voice sings out, "Knock, knock."

"Neenee!" I jump to my feet and rush over. Poppa's there too, and I hug them both. The nurse bustles out the door around us, and the temperature in the room plummets. It's chilly, as if an outside door has blown open.

Neenee says, "Hello, Joelle."

Jo continues to read the newspaper. She flips a page. Without glancing up, she says, "Mrs. Tyler. Mr. Tyler."

Neenee exhales a short breath. "Erin, sweetie." She hustles over to Mom's bedside. Poppa does too. He sets down a vase of red roses, right next to the bouquet of orchids Kerri sent. Jo told me earlier we weren't getting Mom flowers, that it might remind her of funerals. I don't know. I think the flowers add cheerfulness and hope. They look pretty. They're alive.

Neenee presses Mom's face between her hands and kisses her forehead. "How are you feeling, sweetheart?" she asks.

"Fine." Mom's eyes pool with tears. "Daddy." She reaches for his hand.

Jo is suddenly at my side, cupping my elbow. "I guess it's family hour," she says. "We know when we're not wanted, don't we, Nick?" She steers me toward the door.

"Don't go," Neenee calls. "Not on our account. We never get to see you, Nicky. You either, Joelle."

Jo snorts. "Bet you're surprised they even let me up here, aren't you? Since it's family only."

"Stop it, Jo," Mom snaps.

Everyone flinches at the tone of her voice.

Jo goes, "You can stay, Nick. I've got to check on the house. Feed the animals and take out the trash. Maybe I'll bring back our wedding album, Erin. So your parents can see how beautiful you looked that day."

Mom bursts into tears. Jo's face shatters, and she charges out of the room. I feel . . . confused. What was that about?

Jo and Mom never talked about their wedding. I knew they had one, but I didn't know they kept an album. I want to run after Jo, but I'm torn. Conflicted. I need to stay here with Mom. Make her feel better. Lift her spirits.

Under her breath, Neenee says, "How long has it been? Thirteen, fourteen years? We made a mistake. We admit that. She's never going to forgive us for not coming to the wedding, is she?"

Mom asks Neenee for a Kleenex. Poppa shakes his head, looking angry. What Neenee said is filtering through my brain, and I'm remembering that Thanksgiving. Mom explaining to me about people holding grudges, being unforgiving. Did I get it wrong? Is it Jo who's unforgiving?

PART TWO

Jo

My eyelids flutter. Except for the glow of my fish tanks, it's dark in my bedroom. Shadowy. A filmy presence slithers through my field of vision; then a heavy cloth covers my face. I bolt upright, clawing at it. Jo says, "Get dressed. We're going fishing."

I groan, and throw my jeans off my head. On my list of Most Despised Things to Do, fishing earns top spot. Fishing is ranked right above shoveling dog poop from the backyard and playing organized sports in gym. My digital clock reads 4:02. "Do we have to go now? It's the middle of the night."

"I hate to deprive you of your beauty sleep, Cleopatra, but the fish are jumpin' and the cotton is high," Jo replies. "Wear your poncho over your flannel shirt. It's pouring out."

I curse her silently as she creaks out of my room, flipping the switch for the overhead light and blinding me.

*

We're in Beatrice heading down the freeway, and I shiver for the hundredth time. Jo's got the heater blasting, but it doesn't warm my insides. "Where's Mom?" I growl.

"Lost," Jo says. "Trying to find herself. Too bad she forgot to ask me where to look." She checks her armpit.

Now I remember. Mom went on a weekend retreat with Kerri. Ever since her surgery six months ago, Mom's obsessed with all this spirituality stuff. Self-engagement. Integration of body, mind, and spirit. Qigong healing and lojong practice. Jo calls it Buddhist baloney. I think it's weird, but if it makes Mom happy, so what? Her cancer's in remission. That's all I care about. She took me along to her Shambhala meditation class once, and I fell asleep.

"Where are we going?" I ask Jo in a yawn.

"You'll see. I need to talk to you" — Jo lowers her voice — "man to man." She cranks up the volume on this Metallica song "Purify," and I lean against the window to let the guitar riff thrash my skull. Man to man. Oh boy. I can't wait.

Jo swerves into a KFC drive-through. We order the works: two buckets of original recipe, biscuits, mashed potatoes. Mom'd kill us if she knew. She's into natural foods now. Jo keeps warning her about the toxic levels of soy in her system, which doesn't make Mom laugh. Not much makes Mom laugh anymore. She's real intense.

"Thought we'd head up to Bear Lake and camp overnight," Jo shouts over the metal. Clashing cymbals throb in sync with my headache. The only thing I hate worse than fishing is camping. A triple score for fishing and camping together, in the rain.

"What do you want to talk to me about?" I holler.

Jo looks over and narrows her eyes.

I'm in deep shit. What'd I do?

She exits the highway and squeals to a stop at the bottom of the off ramp. Swiping the gritty window with her sleeve, she peers through the sleeting rain, then signals to hang a right. My headache registers off the Richter scale, so I turn down the radio. Take a breather.

Jo says, "You've got stuff to talk to me about. I figure we'll kill two birds."

I don't know what she means. Except . . . I do. How does she know I've been wanting to discuss this problem? It's like she can read my mind. At the moment, I wish she'd read my burning desire to bail and go back to bed.

"No hurry." Jo swerves to avoid a sinkhole in the road. "We've got the whole wet weekend."

I groan again and shrivel inside my poncho.

✳

We rent an outboard at Jake's Boats and stow our gear under the seat. At the Bear Lake Bait and Tackle, Jo buys a bucket of minnows and a can of worms. I hear the owner tell her it's a little early in the year for largemouth, but she might try the north shore, around the rocks. Jo asks, "What about crappie? They biting yet?" He tells her some, but she'll need short shank hooks and jigs. He tells her she'll have to troll pretty deep.

While they're discussing rod weights and hooks, I leaf through the fish magazines. There's a cool photo spread on rainbow sharks. I wonder how they'd do with my Gouramis and loaches. The Red Tail sharks I had for a while were so aggressive they terrorized a whole tank. I never saw them kill, but I'd isolate them in a separate tank before I put my docile fish at risk again. "Oh, hey, good idea." Jo sneaks up behind me. She pulls out a plastic-covered *Playboy* and searches the shelf over my head for another. She locates a *Penthouse*. I'm too embarrassed to accompany her to the cash register.

The rain's stopped by the time we shove off. In the east, the sun's peeking over a jagged ridge, rippling the sky with orange and pink and aqua waves. The only sound is the steady *putt, putt, putt* of our outboard.

Jo keeps looking at me. What? Whatever it is, she's enjoying this. Enjoying making me miserable. I'm not totally, but I'd never give her the satisfaction of knowing that. The dawning day, the waking lake. It's awesome.

Jo slices an index finger across her throat, and I cut the motor. We rock for a moment, then drift. Jo baits a hook and hands me a rod.

As I cast out, she says in a hushed voice, "Keep the lure moving. Watch your bobber."

I scoff. "I know what I'm doing."

"Oh yeah. I forgot. You know it all, Einstein."

Glad to hear she acknowledges my superior intellect. The

lake reflects the wash of watercolor sky, and I lean over to see if it'll reflect me too. Jo says, "Open your mouth a little wider and they'll jump in."

I ignore her. I note my headache's gone.

It's peaceful. We're the only fishing boat on the lake; the only people alive in the world. That's what I imagine. Jo and I are the last two human beings on Earth. Not excluding Mom, but she hates to fish even more than I do — if that's possible.

Jo gets a nibble and yelps. "Whoa. This is no crappie!" Her eyes are wild. She reels in a monster — a two-, maybe three-pound largemouth bass. She's so excited, I reach over and give her a knuckle knock.

Jo holds up the fish. "What do you think? Abigail?"

"That hummer's gotta be a male," I say. "Abernathy."

"Abernathy?" Jo curls a lip. "God. He's gonna get razzed." She unhooks the fish's jaw and lets him slither down her fingers back into the lake. I'm glad we're only catching and releasing, but I still think a hook in the lip has to hurt. Through cupped hands, Jo calls, "Tell them to call you Abe."

Jo baits her hook again and casts out. As she's trolling, she says softly, "We need to talk about sex, Nick."

"Again?" I yawn. "What do you want to know?"

Jo answers, "Are you having any?"

My cheeks flare. "Like I'd tell you."

She fixes on me. She's serious.

"No," I tell her. "And it's not because I don't know how."

She snorts. "Oh, I'm sure you've got the technique down. I saw some of that porno shit you printed off the Internet."

I cough. It's not entirely faked. If she saw all of it, everything from my trash can . . . "Am I gay?" I blurt.

"What?" Jo's eyes enlarge. She looks stunned. She stops
trolling and wedges her rod between the slats in her seat.
Leaning forward, elbows on knees, she gazes deep into my
eyes. "You tell me," she says.

I look away and swallow hard. This is the question I've
been asking myself. Am I? I'm pretty sure of the answer,
but this thing, it's eating me, it's making me have doubts.
"There's this guy in my bio class who . . ." This is hard.
"Who . . ." Too hard.

"Who you have the hots for?" Jo sounds surprised.

I shake my head. "No. I don't. But I think he does for me."

"Oh." Her eyes bulge. "You haven't led him on or anything, have you?"

"No. Geez. What do you think I am?" I yank my line.
Phantom bite. "He knows I'm not interested. At least, I
think he knows. He just got the wrong idea about me."

Jo's head tilts. "How'd that happen?"

I lick my lips. I wish I'd brought ChapStick. I wish I
could phantom myself out of this conversation. "I get called
fag a lot," I tell her.

She sits back. "Kidding, you mean. Like 'Hey, fag.'
'You're so gay.' That kind of thing?"

"Yeah, usually. But sometimes . . ." I swallow. "Sometimes they're not kidding." Methodically, I reel in my line.

"Maybe it's that sissy ponytail you wear." Jo shoots out a
hand and tugs it.

I wrench away. I like my hair long, and so do the girls. "Kids have been calling me gay since kindergarten," I tell her. "Since 'Dickless Nicholas.'"

She starts. "You still remember that?"

I shrug. Some things you never forget.

She watches me tie a chartreuse fly onto my hook. Crappies flock to chartreuse, for some reason. Most animals are color blind. Bees, I read somewhere, seem to be attracted to ultraviolet yellow. I think there's a color spectrum beyond anything humans can see. It makes sense. Animals are ten times more sensitive than we are to natural phenomena like light and sound. Anyway, I hate killing minnows if we're catching and releasing. I hate hurting fish, period.

"You think they assume you're gay because your mom and I are?"

I widen my eyes at her. Duh.

Jo gazes over my head, across the lake. A long, slow breath escapes from her mouth. "We never meant for you to — you know — carry our burden."

"I know," I say. "Forget it."

"We both just wanted kids so bad. We wanted you. I figured you took some crap, but you never complained about it, never told me you were being bullied or harassed. Are you?"

I open my mouth to answer, then shut it. Not bullied in the way she means. Nothing physical. Or threatening. More subtle. The feeling of being different, being looked at in a judgmental way. People drawing conclusions about me based on my moms.

Jo touches my knee. "You would've told me if there was a problem, right? You would've come to me." Her eyes seek mine and linger. "Right?"

"Right," I say. "There's no problem. Nothing I can't handle."

She nods. "People can be cruel. We thought we could protect you. Shelter you from the world, you know? Stupid. Naïve. I'm sorry, Nick. I'm sorry it's been hard for you."

"It hasn't. It's no big deal," I tell her. It's not her fault. I think she needs to hear this. "It's just sometimes . . . I wonder. Since you and Mom are gay, does that mean I am? I read it's in the genes. Like, inherited. Am I going to turn gay someday?" My bobber dips below the surface, and I automatically jerk my rod. I snag something. "Hey, got one," I announce.

As I reel in a fish, Jo's smiling. "I don't think you're gay, Nick. If you were, you wouldn't be wondering about it. You wouldn't be asking me. You'd know. And it's not, like, lying dormant in your system, ready to spring on you."

Her words send a ripple of warmth through me. I didn't think I was, but it's nice to have confirmation.

"What are you going to do about this other guy?" she asks. "Pull up. Pull your line."

I jerk my rod. "Tell him I'm not a fag wad like him."

Jo smacks me upside the head.

"I'm kidding. God."

She pokes me in the chest. "Be kind, all right? He's going to have a hard enough time. He probably already is. I bet he'd appreciate having you for a friend."

My fish breaks the surface while I consider that. Could I be his friend without people thinking I was gay? No. Should I care what people think? No.

But I do.

"So you know all about sex," Jo cuts into my thoughts. "Gay sex? Straight sex? You've seen it all?"

"Pretty much. What do you think?" I hold up my catch. "Butch or Beauregard?"

Jo clicks her tongue. "Definitely Beauregard. He looks a little swishy to me." She cocks a wrist. "Send him home, Saint Nicholas." Her bobber sinks, and she retrieves her rod from under her foot. Standing, she reels in her line.

As I unhook his jaw, carefully, and toss Beauregard back, Jo sits again. "False alarm," she says. She spears her pole through the slats and reaches under the seat. "I guess I might as well junk these girlie 'zines if you're not interested."

I snatch them away from her. "It's going to be a long weekend."

She laughs. "Don't tell your mother. If she knows I'm filling your mind with filth, she won't let us play together anymore." Jo yawns and stretches her arms out to the side. "Time for breakfast." She retrieves the tubs of KFC, breaks into one, and hands me a drumstick. "We *are* going to talk about sex this weekend," she says, digging around and plucking out a wing. "I want you to know the facts about straight sex and gay sex and lesbian sex and any other kind of sex you can think of." She strips meat off the bone with her teeth. "I take that back." She chews and swallows. "If you're thinking about any other kind of sex, you're one sick puppy."

I fake a pant at her.

"But mostly we're going to talk about love." Her eyes deepen. "Because sex without love is wrong, Nick. I want you to understand that. Sex is more than just a physical act. It means something, something special. It's the most beautiful expression of love two people can share."

I stick out my tongue in a gag. I think about Sasha McLaren and how I feel about her. I wonder, not for the first time, if I'm in love with her. I might be, but I'll never know. That dance I missed last September was my Last Chance Dance. Two weeks later, Sasha's dad got transferred or something and she moved to Oregon.

Jo's talking, waving her wing around, and I realize I've tuned out half her sermon. "It doesn't matter who you love — a guy, a girl — love is love. And it's the most important thing in the world. If you have love in your life, you have everything." Jo tosses her greasy bone into the lake.

I say, "I still don't have Xbox."

She just looks at me. "May I continue?"

"You will anyway."

"Sex," she says, "is this total giving of yourself to another person. Think about that. Don't give yourself away too easily." She digs in the bucket and comes up with the biscuits. "And before you even *think* about having sex with a girl, love her enough to marry her. Respect her and cherish her and treat her like a goddess. Because that's what girls are,

Nick. Your role in life, as the inferior sex, is to worship us, obey us, and indulge our every whim."

"Bite me," I mutter. I gnaw on my drumstick.

Without warning, she attacks me. She grabs the straps of my life vest and yanks me off my seat. Before I can react she has me pinned to the bottom of the boat and she's on me. She's smashing a biscuit in my mouth. I'm flailing and trying to free my arms, and her face looms inches away from mine as she snarls, "One more thing, sissy miss. Most girls could beat the crap out of you, and don't you forget it. You're a geek and a wuss." She twists the biscuit until it crumbles, then blows chicken breath on my face.

"Get the hell off me."

Jo slugs my arm. "Don't say 'hell.'"

I say the F word and we have a biscuit battle to the death.

✳

I saved a chartreuse fly from that trip. And the Playboy *centerfold, which reminded me of Sasha — from the neck up. I didn't think I'd be exploring her lower regions. I elevated fishing with Jo to my list of Tolerable Things to Do. Jo said I should live more in the moment, and I tried. I try. But it's only in retrospect that you appreciate the best times you ever had. You know?*

Mom

Neenee and Poppa rent a clubhouse to celebrate Mom's graduation from law school. Hordes of people come. Aunt Liz and Uncle Derrick, my cousins and their girlfriends or wives and kids, friends of Mom's from school and work. Mom looks totally cool in her cap and gown. I can't remember the last time she smiled and laughed so much. She links her arm in mine and leads me over to the gazebo. "Let's get some shots of the two of us together," she says.

Jo's in charge of recording The Big Day. She bought a camcorder for the occasion. "Hold up the diploma," she instructs Mom. "Okay. Now let Nick wear the cap."

Mom sighs wearily, but removes the bobby pins and positions the cap on my head. It fits me perfectly. I think someday I'll be wearing my own cap and gown. Recording my own Big Day. Maybe I'll even go to law school.

Nah. I still want to be an ichthyologist. Make that a

marine biologist. For getting straight A's this semester, Mom and Jo bought me all the equipment to start a saltwater aquarium. Jo took me down to Fish Haven, and we picked out a pair of Barbour's sea horses. We stocked the tank with damselfish and chromis, even some brain coral. It's expensive to keep up, but Jo's got this job at FedEx now that pays good.

I'm as tall as Mom. When she turns and smiles, we're eye to eye. Mom rests her temple against mine, and I feel her happiness flow through me. "Enough, Jo." She holds up a hand. "I better go say hello to all these people." She gives me a squeeze around the middle before floating off toward the clubhouse.

Jo and I hit the refreshment table, then wander over to the chaises by the pool. We settle in. The sun makes my freckles swell. It's a perfect Saturday, a perfect May Day, I think, as I dig out my clip-on sunglasses. Jo slides her shades on and rolls up her sleeves, exposing the dragon tattoo on her left arm. It was her present to herself for "slaying her personal dragons," she says. "For going straight and sober." She'd winked at me. "Not that straight." The tattoo is awesome. I'm hoping she'll let me get one this summer.

"Well, isn't this cozy?" Jo says, lifting the camcorder to her face. I glance over to see what she's filming. It's Mom carrying a flute of champagne over to the French doors through which Kerri is emerging. Kerri leans over and kisses Mom on the cheek. She says something in Mom's ear, and Mom laughs.

Jo lowers the camera for a moment and I see her jaw

clench. She doesn't like Kerri. I'm not sure why, but the feeling is contagious. Mom sips her champagne and laughs again. I think she's a little drunk. Behind Kerri, Neenee flutters out of the clubhouse, smiling. Kerri gives Neenee a hug and a kiss on the cheek too.

Beside me Jo mutters, "Excuse me while I puke."

✳

We leave the party before Mom does. I don't know what time she gets home. All I remember is waking up in the middle of the night feeling tense. Worried. It scares me when they're not both home at night. I'm thirsty so I wander out to the kitchen for a glass of water. In the glow of moonlight through the living room curtains, I see Jo asleep on the sofa. There's a bottle of champagne in her hand, clutched to her chest between her boobs. The foil seal is intact. On the coffee table beside her is the graduation present we got Mom. A maroon leather briefcase with her monogram stitched on the handle: EAT. Erin Alicia Tyler. Jo wanted to add underneath: ME. But I wouldn't let her. The box hasn't been unwrapped yet.

"What do you need, Nick?"

I jump. I didn't realize she was awake. "Nothing," I say. I move a little closer to Jo. She's still dressed for the party. "You okay?"

"Oh sure. I'm great. I'm sensational." She presses her head into the pillow to smile up at me. "Everything's just hunky dory."

I don't like the sound of her voice. Or that smile. The deadness in her eyes. "I was just going to get a drink," I say. "You want something?"

She lets out a short laugh. "I want you to get this out of my sight." She swings the champagne bottle over her head. "Throw it in the trash or pour it down the sink. I don't care. I don't even want to be tempted."

I take it from her. I have the urge to say something like, "Want to go shoot paintball? Drive to the woods? Want to go work off the pain?" But I don't know what pain she's in, exactly. I only feel it. I open my mouth to say, Want to talk about it? but she rolls into a ball, murmuring, "G'night, Nicky. Sweet dreams."

Mom and Jo

I have everything planned for Mother's Day. I'll get up early, prepare their favorite Sunday brunch, and treat them to a movie. I've been saving my allowance for a month. Jo's crazy for my pecan sticky rolls, and Mom likes granola with blueberries and yogurt. The dough for the rolls has to rise before they wake up. I'll blend strawberry smoothies too. I'll set the table with our best dishes; separate the newspaper. Sports and comics for Jo. Business and Living Well for Mom.

Mother's Day is big around our house. My moms don't let me forget it. Jo usually starts dropping hints around the first of May. This year I don't need reminders. We've been through a lot these last few months, and I'm grateful to have both my moms. My mom is a cancer survivor. This Mother's Day is going to be special.

The kitchen is dark and drafty. As I switch on the overhead

light, I find Jo sitting straight-legged on the floor, her back against the dishwasher. Lucky 2's head is in her lap.

I whimper. Jo turns her head and blinks up at me. "She's gone. She died in her sleep."

We knew it was coming, but like Jo says, "You're never prepared for death. You have to make every day of your life count."

I crouch down to hug Lucky 2, to say goodbye. Then the floodgates burst apart and I burrow into Lucky 2's furry side, bawling my eyes out. Jo smoothes my hair. She's crying too. She tries to comfort me, to tell me how special Lucky 2 is — or was — and how we're the lucky ones to have had her. I know all that. But it helps for Jo to say it.

When we're both cried out, I stand and head for the stairs. "I'll go tell Mom."

"She's not here." Jo swipes her sleeve across her nose.

"Where is she?"

Jo continues to stroke Lucky 2, not answering. She stares into the cold, empty kitchen, and so do I. I know where Mom is. I wish I didn't.

✳

We bury Lucky 2 under the linden tree. She won't be alone. There's my first Kuhli loach and the clownfish and Gouramis. I bury every fish, to honor them, their lives, and what they brought to mine. We've saved a spot for Savage, but I don't even want to think about him dying. That'll kill Mom.

As Jo tamps the burial mound with a shovel, Mom closes

her eyes and bows her head. She got home around seven this morning. When I told her Lucky 2 was gone, she collapsed in a heap on the floor. Her face is still blotchy, and she's clutching a fistful of Kleenex. I know she's praying for Lucky 2. If there is a God, I thank Him, or Her, for all the good times we had together, all the years. A lock of Lucky 2's fur is in my pocket to keep as a memento.

Next to me Jo props the shovel under her armpit and blows a wet bubble of air between her lips. She does it again. It sounds like . . .

Mom and I blink at Jo. Then I get it. I laugh. Jo continues bubble farting.

Mom isn't laughing. "You have no respect," she snarls at Jo. Pointing to the grave, she adds, "That dog gave us the best years of her life and you make a mockery of it."

Jo stops blowing. Her face steels. She gazes across the mound at Mom and says, "Don't talk to me about respect, Erin. Don't you dare talk to me about respect. Or making a mockery of the best years of anyone's *life*."

As if slammed by a fist, Mom stumbles backward. A chasm opens. It's been widening for weeks now, maybe months. I can't slow the rupture. I can't repair the rip. I leap onto the mound, extend my arms in either direction to close the gap. "Can we get another dog?" I ask. "Please? We need a dog." I look from Jo to Mom.

Mom shakes her head.

I clap my hands together in prayer. "Please?" To Jo. "Pretty please?" To Mom. I press my fingers to my chin and plead.

Mom wraps her arms around herself. She says the same thing she always does: "No more animals." Turning, she pads back toward the house.

Jo and I watch her retreat.

"We need a dog, Jo," I tell her. "We could convince Mom, I know we could. We'll get one from the pound."

"Not now, Nick," she says.

"A needy dog," I go on. "An old one."

Jo stabs the shovel into the ground. She kicks a dirt clod, then veers off toward the garage.

"A blind one," I call. "Or deaf. One with missing parts." Jo's going to leave, probably be gone all day. "I bet they have a crippled one. A quadriplegic."

I want to chase her. Chase Mom. Lock them in a room together. Tie them up, bind them, make them talk, work it out.

But I can't. I can't move. The earth won't budge, and my feet are stuck.

On Lucky 2's grave, I sink to my knees. "Come back to us," I say. I pray. "Don't leave us like this." It's Mother's Day. I have everything planned.

Mom

Something's wrong. It's too quiet. From the hallway, I fling my backpack into my room, pass through the kitchen, and thump up the stairs.

Mom spins around and gives a little yelp. "Nick, my God." She presses a hand to her heart. "You scared me. What are you doing home already?"

"It's a teacher in-service day," I tell her.

"Oh." She frowns. "I forgot. Did I know?"

My eyes skitter around the room. Something's different.

Mom says, "I wanted to have this done before you got home. But since you're here, would you mind giving me a hand?" She hitches her chin toward the bed.

That's when I realize she's moving furniture. The tall dresser is positioned in the middle of the long south wall, where it wouldn't have fit yesterday because that's where the bookcase was. It's been moved over by the closet, where the cedar chest was. I don't see the cedar chest.

"I want to move the bed over there under the window." Mom clutches the right rear post. "Help me push?"

"What'd you do with the cedar chest?" I ask. "And the TV?" The little portable TV I like to watch when I'm home sick. When Jo lets me come up here and crash. The TV's gone.

Mom gets impatient. She grunts with the effort it takes to budge the bed. The frame's heavy. It's oak, four-poster. They've had this bed as long as I can remember. As long as I've been alive. When Mom doesn't reply, I repeat, "Where are they?"

She exhales exasperation. "Jo took them," she says.

"Where?"

Mom straightens and sighs. "Sit down, Nick. I need to tell you something."

My heart rips. A black hole opens up.

My first thought, my only thought is, No.

Mom perches on the mattress and pats the spot next to her. "We should've had this talk a long time ago."

I stay where I am, arms limp at my sides.

Mom pulls a loose tendril of hair over her head and tucks it back into her ponytail. "Jo left," she says. "We split up."

The synapses in my brain spark, misfire, disconnect. An electrical storm shorts out my consciousness. Still, the news seeps in.

One word escapes my mouth. "Why?" It hovers, as if suspended in space.

Mom wipes away the sweat on her forehead. "It wasn't . . ." She expels a short breath. "It didn't work." She hesitates and peers up at my face. She can't hold my eyes. "We weren't good for each other anymore."

"You were good for me."

"Oh, Nick." Mom stands. Her arms reach out, but I back away. I stumble, stagger. To the wall. The closet. I wrench it open. Jo's half is empty. I slam the door.

"Where is she?" I say. I screech, "Where!" I don't give Mom time to answer. I storm down the stairs. To the garage.

I fling open the door.

Beatrice is gone. All our tools. The paintgun. No.

No!

"Where is she?" I shrill at Mom, who's in the kitchen pouring herself a glass of iced tea.

She startles and spills tea on the floor as she closes the refrigerator door. "I don't know," she says, grabbing a sponge from the sink. She mops up her mess. "She said she'd call you later."

I charge into the living room. The furniture in there has been rearranged too. Things are missing. Pictures. The CD player — it's gone. I run to my room. Everything's the same. Except . . . it's not.

Everything's changed.

✳

The phone rings, and I cover my ears. I'm never talking to her. Never. My door is barricaded with my body, my hunched-over rock-hard body. The roaring in my head makes me dizzy, and I squeeze my knees to my chest to anchor myself.

Mom's voice is soft, but I can hear her through the door frame. "Yeah, he surprised me. I forgot he only had a half day today. What?"

She listens.

"No, not tonight," she answers. "He needs time. We need time alone."

No, we don't. I scrabble to my feet and fling open the door; stalk to the kitchen. I'm going to cuss Jo out so bad. Mom too. Tell them what liars they are. They promised. Jo broke her word. She's a liar and a coward. They both are. How could she just up and leave without telling me? Without *taking* me.

As I round the corner, Mom says, "Thanks, Kerri. I don't know what I'd do without you." In a lower voice, an intimate voice, she murmurs, "Me too."

The dizziness returns, and I wobble. I clutch the table for support. Mom sees me and smiles. "Hey, you want me to call Papa John's and have them deliver? You can get pepperoni. I'll just close my eyes and pretend it's tofu."

I say the first thing that burbles to the surface. "Go to hell."

Mom's eyes balloon. She comes at me.

As I'm fleeing, she catches my shirtsleeve. "Nick." Her fingernails dig into my arm. "None of this is your fault."

I whirl on her. "I didn't think it was." I wrench away. "You're the one who screwed it up. You ruined everything."

Her face looks stricken. Sick.

So what? I slam my bedroom door in her face.

✳

I waited. I waited all night. The phone never rang. That house was a ghost ship. No inhabitants. No music. No TV. No certainty my door would open a crack and she'd stick her head in. "Goodnight, Nick. Sweet dreams." I didn't know where her head was.

Jo was gone. For good. I knew it; felt it in my gut. I stared into water, ocean, my saltwater tank. The undulating coral, mesmerizing repetitive motions and movements of fish, back and forth, back and forth.

I closed my eyes and wished. I wished so hard my chest hurt. My teeth hurt. I wished for Jo to keep her promise, for time to turn around. Go back. I wished for bones that didn't break, or hearts, or homes. Or people.

Mom

She knocks on my door. "Nick, you're going to be late. I'm leaving in ten minutes."

Go to hell, I think. Go away.

It's been the same every morning for a week. She stands at my door. Lingers. I hear her breathing. Dragon fire. A thick slab of wood separates us. Physically, anyway. "Nick?"

Silence.

Finally, she clues in.

A few minutes later the front door closes and locks.

She doesn't know I've been up and dressed for hours, waiting. Waiting for her to leave. For the phone to ring.

I'm hungry, so I wander into the kitchen. Overnight the poltergeists moved objects again. The coffeemaker is at the edge of the counter. The toaster is missing. Cobwebs cling thick on the ceiling.

I can hang around here all day, but it's too creepy. And

boring. At least at school there's math and biology, motion, noise, distraction.

I walk the halls in a vegetative state. No one talks to me, no one tries to engage my senses. Which isn't unusual. I don't really have any friends. Besides Jo. This girl in English smiles occasionally, and last week I was considering maybe smiling back, nodding. I wondered if she'd think I was hitting on her, or recognize the possibility. But not now. The thrill is gone, as Jo would say.

I hate girls.

When I get home there's a message on our voice mail. My heart pounds as I punch in the code to retrieve it.

"Hi, honey. I'm just calling to check on you. Make sure you got to school. I might have to work late —"

I hang up. Who cares?

✳

Thursday morning Mom tricks me. I hear the front door close, but when I emerge she's standing in the living room. She ambushes me. "How long are we going to play this game?" she asks.

Shut up, I think. I step back into my room. She lurches and snags my backpack. Which I drop at her feet. And shut the door.

"Nick." Her hand slaps the wood. "Goddammit." She pounds the door. "Talk to me."

Now? *Now* you want to talk?

I stare at the door. My eyes bore holes into the wood. I

conjure up my pyrokinetic powers to burst the door into flames.

"It's not my fault she hasn't called," Mom says. "I think you should be prepared for the possibility she may never call."

"Shut up!" I explode out the door. "She'll call!" My hands grip Mom's shoulders and I push her back, back into the living room. She's against the fireplace and I'm in her face. "She'll call." We're eye to eye. I want to hurt her. I want to hit my mother where it hurts.

I drop my arms. I'm shaking visibly. A tremor rumbles under my feet and knocks me off balance. I stumble, grope for substance, solid ground. Any hope to hang on to.

My pack. I grasp it by the front pocket and head out the door.

She doesn't chase after me. She doesn't yell or call my name or say something stupid like, "Let's talk about this."

Too late, Mom. Too late.

Lucky 3

I'm in the middle of an algebra test when the intercom blares: "Nicholas Tyler to the office." I freak. Not because everyone's looking at me. No one gets called to the office unless it's an emergency. I'm rattled. Should I leave my stuff? There's only ten minutes left in class. Mr. Wagner, the teacher, says from his desk in back, "Bring your test to me."

I was on the last problem anyway. I gather my papers, my scratch sheet, and backpack. Wagner looks pissed. "Leave quietly." He hates disruptions. Hustling down the hall, I'm thinking, They found the body. That's why she didn't call, because she rolled Beatrice in a ditch and she's been dead for a week, and nobody knew. Nobody cared.

I care. I should've called the cops and reported a missing person. Mom should've called. She should've cared.

Then Jo's standing there, loitering in the front hall, jingling her keys. When she sees me, a smile streaks across her face.

I don't smile. I stop dead in my tracks. I want to run to her, throw my arms around her, cry for happiness. I want to run from her, leave her, abandon her the way she did me.

I will them to, but my feet can't stay planted. One moves, then the other. They slog ahead. Forward. In front of her, they stop.

Jo's smile disappears. She twirls her key ring on her index finger. "Go ahead and say it."

"I hate you."

Her eyes fill with tears. "Yeah. I don't blame you. I messed up." She sniffs. "Story of my life."

This makes me so mad I explode. "Am I supposed to feel sorry for you or something? Am I supposed to *forgive* you? Pretend nothing ever *happened* and we're all buddy-buddy again?" My eyes sting, and my face is burning hot. Fists ball at my sides.

Jo smirks. "Pretty much."

"Well, fuck you!" My voice reverberates off the walls. The urge to hit her is strong. But she'll beat the crap out of me. Instinctively, I fling my backpack at her, narrowly missing her thick skull.

"Hey!" she yells, dodging the missile, then grabbing my wrist. "What the hell is wrong with you?"

"What is going on out here?" Mrs. Mendoza, the vice principal, barrels out of her office. She nearly trips on my backpack.

Jo lets go of me and spins around. "Sorry. Uh, minor family squabble." She retrieves my pack and, shrugging at Mrs. Mendoza, says, "Can you believe the foul mouths on kids these days? I don't know where he gets it. Must be at school because we don't allow that kind of language at home."

"Bullshit," I hiss under my breath. "What home?"

Jo flinches. To Mrs. Mendoza she says, "Can you believe a kid would talk to his mother that way?"

"You're not my mother."

Jo fixes on me and holds my eyes. I have to look away.

Mrs. M looks baffled. She's speechless, for once. Jo loops an arm around my shoulders and clamps down on my upper arm. "We'll just continue this discussion outside." She smacks me in the chest with my backpack and steers me toward the door.

"Hold on." Mrs. M quick-steps in front of us. She blocks the door with her massive bulk. "Could I see some identification? I'll need proof you're his mother." She scans Jo up and down.

"Proof?" Jo clicks her tongue. "What do you mean? Like, stretch marks?" She chuckles, sort of nervously, and rolls her eyes at me.

"I'm required to check our files in the office before you leave with him." Mrs. M studies Jo. She orders us, "Follow me, please," and reaches for my arm.

I lurch away. "She's my mother," I tell her. I huff for effect.

The bell rings, and instantly we're swallowed in a tsunami of students, all shrieking and rushing for the doors. We lose ourselves in the squall. Out on the front walk, Jo says in my ear, "Who stuck a burr up her butt?"

I don't answer. I grind my teeth. I'm still mad enough to beat her bloody, but she's here, at least. At last. My anger morphs into relief. As we head for the parking lot, I say, "What are you doing, kidnapping me?"

"Yeah, sure." She unlocks the passenger door on Beatrice and swings it open for me. "Kidnapping includes ransom. Who'd pay a friggin' dime to get *you* back?"

I show her my tongue. She slams the door behind me and climbs in on her side.

"Where have you been?" I ask.

She acts like she doesn't hear.

"Where!" I shout.

Jo turns and looks at me. "Away," she says finally. "Dealing."

"That's not good enough."

"Well, it'll have to be," she snaps. "It's not always about you, okay? I had some shit to work through. You think this is easy for me? Give me a break, will you?" She looks ready to cry. Beatrice splutters to life, and Jo backs out of her space. We pull out of the parking lot, and I drag my eyes away from her. For a moment.

I ask, "Where are we going?" Home, I hope. This was all a bad dream. A sitcom episode. In the side view mirror, I watch Morey Middle School diminish in the distance.

Jo answers, "To our new place."

She must feel my spike of joy because she adds, "Don't get excited. It's no movie star mansion."

The understatement of the century, I discover, when we pull into a crappy apartment complex twenty minutes later. Jo drives under a dilapidated carport.

There are garbage bags piled to the roof between buildings, and it stinks. I plug my nose as I get out. Jo's suddenly at my side, guiding me toward the stairwell. "Your grand-parents always figured me for white trash," she says. "I guess they got that right."

I don't know how to respond. Am I supposed to feel sorry for her? I can't when I'm feeling sorry for myself.

"I can see you're so stoked over this deal you're wetting your pants," Jo says. "The exterior's just a front. Wait'll you see the inside. Think Trump Towers."

I follow Jo up the rickety steps. Her apartment's on the second floor, halfway down a concrete walkway. She inserts a key in a door and screaks it open. An enormous dog leaps out at us, barking and drooling. I grab the doorknob to keep from being leveled.

"Down, boy," Jo orders the dog. It obeys, and sniffs my crotch. Jo rolls her eyes. "Men."

The dog takes an emergency leak off the landing. I hope there's no one underneath. With a sweep of her arm, Jo motions me inside.

"What's his name?" I ask. As I venture one step over the threshold, the dog bears down my back to beat me inside.

Jo cocks her head at me. "Well, he was first in line for death row at the pound, so take a guess."

I laugh. It feels good to laugh.

Jo says, "Okay, so this is the skybox."

The apartment is cramped. Dingy. The one curtain on the window is falling off the rod. Boxes and trash bags climb to the popcorn ceiling. It's been more than a week and she hasn't unpacked anything. This feeling comes over me; it overwhelms me. It's . . . ease. Comfort. Even safety.

Jo swings open a door at one end of the room. "Oh my God!" she gasps. "We have a bathroom." She slams the door. "Don't tell the landlord. He'll raise the rent."

I slug her as she passes by. She slugs me back, then punches on the CD player. Metallica bursts my eardrums.

"What?" Jo yells.

"What what?" I yell back.

"That sappy smile on your face."

I try to wipe it off, but it's stuck. For the first time all week my stomach doesn't hurt and I'm not on the verge of tears. A bass riff claws at my cortex and slithers down my trachea.

Jo crosses to the banged-up refrigerator and wrenches it open. "Let's see. We've got leftover Chinese," she hollers, "and rock-hard pizza. Or your favorite, chicken wings."

My stomach grumbles. "That's it?"

"Hey, my gourmet chef bailed on me." She shuts the fridge.

"No, I didn't!" I scream. "You left me. You deserted me." Our eyes meet.

"I didn't want to," she yells back. "I —" Trudging over, she twists down the volume on the CD player. "I didn't have a choice."

"Yes, you did. You could've stayed."

She shakes her head. "No, Nick. I couldn't."

I know it, but I don't want to believe.

"I stayed as long as I could. You knew what was going on," she says. "I don't need that shit. I don't stay where I'm not wanted."

"You were wanted." I glare at her; soften the look.

She looks away. Her face sags.

I don't want her to cry. I add, "You could've taken me with you, at least. Are you kidding, leaving me alone with the Ice Queen?"

Jo shakes her head at the floor. "You weren't mine to take. And don't disrespect your mother."

"Why not?"

"Because she's your mother."

"But why couldn't you —"

"Because I never adopted you." A plastic bag rustles, and Lucky 3 launches up. He leaps on Jo's front and about knocks her off her feet. Jo scruffs his ears. "You goof," she says.

"What do you mean?" I say again, louder. "Why didn't you adopt me?"

"Because I was trusting, okay? And stupid." Jo pushes Lucky 3 down. "Can we talk about this later?" She heads for the bathroom.

Why would she have to adopt me? She's my mom.

"No, we can't." Now I'm mad. I'm enraged. All the times she made me fight, made me decide what was worth fighting for. I charge her. "Did you even *want* to take me?" I shove her from behind. "Did you?"

"Nah." She swings around. "You didn't mean anything to me." She clenches the tendon on my shoulder and squeezes.

I club her off. I'm not joking. "Why didn't you *fight* for me?"

She opens her mouth, but no words come out.

"Did you even ask?" Because that's what's been bugging me. Killing me. I never once heard Jo ask for me. I never heard her argue with Mom, yell, scream my name, insist,

"Nick is my kid. He's going with me." Aren't I worth fighting for?

Off a TV tray, she picks up an empty McD carton and opens it. A shred of shriveled lettuce inside. She gazes into the depths of the cardboard for seven, eight seconds. I whack it out of her hand. "Answer me."

She lifts her eyes. Her lips part. "I can't fight her for you." Jo's eyes go dead. "I won't."

A rising panic lodges in my chest. "Why? Don't you want me?"

Without warning, Jo crushes me to her. She holds me so hard my spine cracks. "Of course I want you. You know I do."

"Then why?" Why? I choke back tears.

Jo doesn't answer; just holds me and rocks me. We stay that way for a long time. I hang on to her. I never want to let her go.

She wants it too. I know she does. She wants me.

Lucky 3 starts barking. Barking and lunging at us, snagging Jo's sleeve in his teeth. Jo and I separate a little. Stupid dog. I think, Go away. She doesn't need a dog. She needs me.

*

Later, we're sitting on the floor, sorting through CDs. "Some of these are mine, you know," I tell Jo.

"So take them," she says.

"I don't want them. I'm just saying . . ." I scan around the apartment; check it out. "Where do I sleep?" I ask.

She doesn't hear.

"Where —"

"You're not staying."

I start to blow. "But —"

"Your mom doesn't even know you're here. If she did . . ." Jo slices a finger across her neck and makes a slitting sound in her mouth like paper ripping. "I've got to get you home soon."

Home, I think. Where is that now? Here? There? I know where I want it to be. For no reason Lucky 3 scrabbles to his feet and romps through the garbage bags. This dog is mental. He drops a slimy tennis ball into my lap.

Jo says, "I haven't talked to your mom yet about . . . you know, visitation rights. All that crap."

"So call her." I lob the tennis ball toward the kitchen, and Lucky 3 bounds after it. He slides across the linoleum and crashes into the stove, then gets his paw stuck in a pizza box and drags it across the room. It makes us both laugh. Dumb dog, I think. Retard. Okay, I already love this dog.

"I can't talk to her yet," Jo says. She pries open a CD case to check if there's a disc inside. Most of them are empty. The ones that aren't contain mismatched CDs. "Besides, I don't have a phone. I'm getting one. It's scheduled for installation on Monday, supposedly."

"I'll talk to Mom and call you. Then you can come and get me." Summer vacation starts in ten days. I hadn't been looking forward to it until now. I'll stay here with Jo. We'll do all the stuff we used to do, like fish and spar at the gym and go target practice. My marker's propped in the corner, I see. It's globbed with paint. We'll rent movies and slum at the mall. "Do you have a pool?" I ask.

"Does Trump Towers have a pool?" She clicks her tongue. "A cesspool." She continues to open and close the CD case. Her knuckles are raw and her hands are chapped. I wonder if she's still working at FedEx. I'm afraid to ask. The look on her face is the same one she had when she told me about Mom's cancer.

"What?" I ask. Nobody died. No one's dying. My Barbour's sea horses have parasites or something, but I can treat them. "You don't want me here, is that it?"

Jo casts me a withering look. "You know that's not it. It's just . . ." She shuts the CD case and pitches it across the room. "If you're here, you're not there."

I widen eyes at her. "Brilliant, Einstein."

She reaches over and smacks me upside the head. "Don't be a smartass."

I catch her wrist and yank. The force topples her over frontward. She throws a headlock on me and we wrestle in the trash. Lucky 3 barks his brains out. Jo and I noogie each other and roll. I pin her to the floor. "Onetwothree." I slap the mat. I leap up and dance around like Rocky, my arms in the air. I come at Jo again.

"Time," she calls, grinding her back into the wall. I slide down beside her. We're both winded. I pick up a magazine from a stack by the TV tray. It's the *Sports Illustrated* swimsuit edition. Jo and I always fight over it.

She says out of nowhere, "What's your philosophy of life, Nick?"

"What? What do you mean?"

"You know what I mean. What do you tell yourself at a time like this? How do you make it through?"

You do what you need to do. Right? It sounds lame, particularly in this situation. Mom's philosophy, ignore it and it'll go away, is even weaker.

Jo goes, "You handle this shit better than me. I need to know what you tell yourself. What's your pick-me-up line?"

I shrug. "I don't know."

"Come on. I need a little inspiration here. My well's run dry. I'd fill it with beer if I hadn't made this regrettable promise to this sorry-ass person who doesn't even have a philosophy of life."

My philosophy? "Life sucks and then you die," I say.

Jo blinks at me. She crunches her head against the wall and starts to shake. She's laughing. Uncontrollably. Except it isn't the kind of laughter that billows up from your belly and disperses in balloons of happiness and joy. The kind that makes you forget how bad things really are and that you're hurting, maybe bleeding, afraid of dying or going away. This laughter is harsh, strident. It hurts to hear.

I squinch my ears and will her to stop. Stop! She goes, "Hoo boy, Nicky." She slaps my bent knees and pushes to her feet. "Let's go rustle up some grub."

She waits for me at the door, but I don't move. I can't. I can't tear my eyes away from the object in Lucky 3's mouth.

It's one of Jo's grizzly bear slippers, all ratty and ripped. I didn't know she kept those.

Out of this river inside me a tear sluices down my cheek. Then another. I'm bawling, and Jo's cradling my head in her chest and shielding me with her body, and she's crying too. Tears are gushing from my eyes and I'm sobbing so hard I'm hiccuping. Jo's wailing. Jo's leaking more than me.

After we soak each other in tears, we sit for a while, re-covering.

Jo speaks aloud the words I can't form: "God. I never knew anything could hurt this much."

Mom

She runs a yellow light, her eyes shooting flames and her mouth crimped, so I know she's pissed. Good. She had no right. She didn't even ask what I wanted.

We pull into the garage, into the vacant space left by Beatrice. There's only dust and cobwebs where the tools used to be. Empty hooks for fishing gear. A busted shovel. The garage is haunted. The whole house is haunted.

Mom gets out and leaves me in the car. Fine. I'll live in here.

She's standing by the sink, drinking a bottled water when I stumble in a minute later. The empty garage creeps me out.

"I'm not proud of you." The first words she's spoken since we left Neenee and Poppa's.

I want to say, Yeah? Well, I'm not proud of you either.

My pits are soaked and my hands are clammy. It's hot, sweltering. The air conditioning in the car is busted, and

Jo's not here to fix it. I want a soda, but Mom's giving off venomous vibes, and I'm not walking past her.

"I thought we had a deal." Her eyes cut to me.

"*You* did," I say. "You never asked me."

Mom drops a jaw. "We discussed all the options. Where were you?"

Here, I think. Invisible. Listening to you go, "Blah, blah, blah."

"You didn't want to go to camp and you refused day care at the Y and you couldn't come up with the names of any friends whose parents I would've been happy to call and ask if we could work out a plan for having you stay with them during the day. So we settled on Neenee. You were happy with that."

"No, I wasn't. You were." I hated the idea. A whole month at Neenee and Poppa's? I'd die of boredom. They didn't like me watching TV during the day or playing video games. What was I supposed to do for a whole freaking month? "I hate it there."

Mom scrapes out a chair and sits. She presses the sweating bottle of water against her forehead. I saunter to the fridge for a Coke.

"Who were you calling?" she says, accusingly. She adds under her breath, "As if I didn't know."

Then don't ask, I think. The icy cold fizz in my mouth is a welcome relief. I slug down half the can. I'm hungry too, but I'll eat later. After Mom leaves. After she runs to *her*. I know that's why Mom wanted me gone, so she could be with *her*.

"Did you realize it was long distance? Do you know how much Neenee's phone bill is going to be?"

Like I care. That telephone in the basement was my only link to life. The only human connection keeping me alive.

I feel better now. Calmer. I miss my fish. She'd better have followed my care and feeding instructions to the letter. As I head for my room, Mom says at my back, "I'm not done talking to you."

Blah, blah, blah. I wonder how my Acropora frag is doing. I should've been here to keep an eye on it. Coral is fragile. I should never have trusted her with the tanks. If she doesn't know how to take care of me, how could she take care of my fish? I go to close my door, but Mom's followed me in and pushes it open. "How many times did she call you?"

Everything looks the same. Neater, maybe. Kerri better not have been in here.

"Nick, I asked you a question."

It's too quiet. Too. Freaking. Quiet. I crank on my stereo full blast.

Mom charges across the room and slaps off the power. "Answer me." She whirls and clenches my limp arms. "Look at me when I'm talking to you." She gives me a shake.

My eyes bore into her chest, her hole. They slowly rise up her neck to her face. "She didn't call me. I called her."

Mom blinks, like she doesn't expect that.

"Why can't I stay with Jo?" I ask. "She's home during the day. She wants me around."

Mom's eyes veil.

Okay, that wasn't fair. I know Mom has to work. But none of this is fair.

I tell Mom, "She's working nights now so she's around in the daytime. There's plenty to do. You wouldn't have to worry about me keeping busy."

Mom pivots and veers toward the door.

I yell, "I'm speaking to you!"

She doesn't even slow. Fine. Be that way. I'll just talk to Jo on the phone all day here.

"I don't like you going there." Mom reappears on the threshold. "I don't appreciate how surly and uncommunicative you are every time you come back from there. And that neighborhood she lives in isn't safe."

Lies. Excuses. Why doesn't she just tell me the truth? I say it for her: "You hate Jo."

Mom affects her classic look: You wouldn't understand.

But I do understand. I'm smart enough to understand, Mom. You're selfish and I hate you.

*

The doorbell rings as I'm dragging to the kitchen for a bag of chips. I feel sluggish. Mom's upstairs, creaking around. The shower just came on.

Whoever's at the door knocks. I know who it is. I don't answer.

The door opens. Why'd she even bother to knock if she has a key?

"Hey, Nick," Kerri says, bounding into the kitchen. "I

didn't know you were back." She sets a vase of flowers on the table.

I don't respond. We're out of chips. When Jo was here we always kept a stash of junk food in the bottom cupboard. Kerri must've found it and told Mom. Or ate it herself.

"You want to come to dinner with us? We're going to that new sushi bar down the street."

I look at Kerri.

Her eyes widen, and she claps a hand over her mouth. "Ooh, sorry. I forgot. You don't do fish, do you?" She rubs a knuckle against her front teeth. "They have teriyaki and rice bowls." Her eyebrows arch. She has penciled brows. Fake brows.

Shut up, I think. You make me sick. Be careful not to touch her, I think as I slip behind and head back to my room. My sanctuary. I've missed it. My tanks, my fish, the soft buzz of lights and whirr of motors. I swear I can hear my fish whispering to me, communicating with me, telling me what they want and need. They're my only company now that Jo's gone. My sole companions, so to speak.

I stretch out on my bed and close my eyes to memorize the feel and sound and smell of my aquariums. I imagine I'm with my fish in the water. Free, untethered. The glass walls dissolve and our space expands, flows to the open ocean. This is the only space I have left here. When Jo moved out, she took more than her stuff. She stripped the soul from this house.

A sharp rap on the door snaps my thoughts back.

What now?

"Nick!"

It's Mom. I roll off the bed, taking my time. I wrench open the door.

Mom startles, like she didn't think I'd come.

Fooled you.

"We're going out to dinner. If you need me, I left the number by the phone." She waggles a stiff finger at me. "Stay off the phone."

I want to break that finger. I eye Kerri behind Mom, rolling her eyes at me. What? We're not in this together. We have nothing together.

Mom adds, "If you get hungry, there's a quiche in the refrigerator that Kerri made."

I'd starve before eating her food. I'd poison myself before I'd be poisoned by her.

Slowly, deliberately, I shut the door in their faces.

Kerri

Savage is dying. Kerri says, "Get your mom on the phone and tell her to meet us at Mesa Vet Clinic. Tell her Sixth and Harlan. It's the closest one I could find to her office."

I don't move. In my arms I hold Savage's limp and lifeless body. I stare at the bloody drool dribbling out his mouth and soaking through the towel.

Kerri sneezes. "Nick, please." She twists away and blows her nose. "She'll want to be there at the end." My brain engages.

The End.

Kerri asks, "Where do you keep your cat carrier? In the garage?"

Carrier? What carrier? Savage never went anywhere, besides the one trip in a duct-taped box from the old house to the new. He's feral — you can't catch him. That's how I knew he was dying. He let me walk right up to him and pick him up. He was on the back stoop, lying on his side, glassy-eyed.

"I'll just carry him," I tell Kerri. I shift the bunched-up towel, and Kerri reaches out like I'm going to drop him. "You call Mom," I tell her. "I have to call Jo."

Kerri acts like she wants to debate this, but the defiance in my voice must change her mind. Good decision. She gets on her cell. One-handed, I flip mine open and punch the speed dial number for Jo.

My cell phone was Kerri's idea, so Mom and I could stay in touch. Right. So if there was an emergency at home, I could call Mom. Sure. The only way Mom agreed to let me stay home by myself was if I called to check in every hour on the hour.

Like that happens.

A few minutes later we're speeding down the freeway. Savage lifts his head once and growls. I say, "It's okay, boy." I gently stroke him with my index finger.

"How long have you had him?" Kerri asks.

Shut up, I think. I hate when she talks to me. We've talked enough already today. In my peripheral vision I notice she's done something different with her hair. It's blue-black except for the bleached blond streaks in front down her face. She thinks she's so cool. She's all pierced. She's a freak.

She sneezes again and digs in her bag. She pulls out a snot rag. "Look, I know how hard this is for you." She blows her nose. "My parents were divorced when I was eight."

"So?"

"So I've been there."

No, you haven't, I scream inside. It's not the same. Is she stupid, or what?

"My dad abandoned us, basically. Just sort of left us for dead. I remember feeling like it was all my fault."

"It probably was," I say. You're so weird. I don't say that.

Kerri's looking at me and her eyes are smiling. "Smart-ass," she goes.

I don't want to joke around with her. She's not Jo. Savage is dying. "Where's Taco?" I say.

Kerri frowns. "What?" She flicks the right turn signal and swerves toward the Harlan Street exit. The traffic is backed up on the off ramp. "Damn," Kerri says. "This had to happen at rush hour."

"Taco," I repeat. "Takashi. Your son. Remember him?" The one you abandoned?

She lays on the horn and merges between two SUVs. She's so hyper it makes me jumpy. "He's not my son. Dammit! Let me in." She bolts forward. "He's Reiko's, and so, naturally, he's with her." Kerri's eyes dart across at me. She bears down on the accelerator. "He never really liked me. We never, you know, bonded." Kerri's cell chirrups. "Would you get that? If it's your mom, tell her we're stuck on Harlan. We're about ten minutes away."

I don't get her phone. I'm not about to dig around in her personal belongings and used snot rags.

The phone rings and rings. Kerri looks at me. I look away. Eventually, she plunges a hand into her purse and retrieves the cell. The ringing's stopped by then. She says, "Reiko and I weren't together all that long. She wasn't into commitment." She tosses the cell on the dash and lays on the horn. "Anyway, I thought Takashi was kind of a spoiled brat. Don't tell him I said that."

Like I see him. That kid was a freak too.

"How's Savage?" Kerri asks.

I finger his head, but he doesn't move. Come on, Savage. Breathe.

We get to the bottom of the ramp, and Kerri hangs a right. She says, "What happened between your mom and Jo wasn't anyone's fault. It happens."

Don't talk to me.

"You think it's my fault, don't you? You blame me."

She's stupid and psychic.

"Look, I don't know what Jo told you —"

"She didn't tell me anything. If you're going to clean our house again don't touch my stuff. Don't use the downstairs bathroom. It's mine. And next time you do my laundry, leave it in the laundry room. Don't come in my room — ever." I adjust Savage on my lap. See if he'll growl, twitch. BREATHE.

I expect Kerri to yell at me or cuss me out or something so I can retaliate. Because I hate her. I hate what she did to us.

She gazes straight ahead. "I'm sorry, Nick," she says. "I know how much it hurts."

I almost throw Savage in her face. She doesn't know. It's not the same and she knows it. "You don't know what hurt is," I say.

She looks all crushed. Faker.

We don't talk the rest of the way.

*

Savage is gone by the time we reach the vet clinic. Mom's there. She rushes over and takes Savage from my arms. "He's dead," I say.

"Oh, honey . . ." She buries her face in the towel. Kerri puts her arms around Mom and touches her head to Mom's. "I'm sorry, babe," she says. Her voice cracks. "I'm so sorry."

Faker. Liar.

Jo isn't here, out front on the sidewalk, or visible through the glass entryway. I go inside and search around the waiting area. No Jo. I cross to a shelf of brochures and wedge behind the potted plant for privacy. I call her.

"Nick," she answers on the first ring. "How is he?"

"Where are you?" I say. "We're at the vet's. Mesa Clinic. You said you knew where it was."

"How is he?" Jo repeats. "Is he . . . ?"

"Dead."

"Oh, Nicky." She exhales audible pain. "Nick."

Now the tears I've been holding back start to gush. I sink into the nearest chair and curl into a knot. "Where are you?" I say again.

"I'm home," Jo answers. Now she's crying too. "How's your mom?"

"Why aren't you here?" I whimper. "I want you here." I clutch the phone tighter to my ear.

"I know. I know. I just . . . I can't. Not yet. I'm sorry, Nick. I can't be where she is. How is she? Erin? Your mom, how's she taking it?"

I rubberneck around the plant. Mom and Kerri are near the reception desk, nodding at a woman in green scrubs who's got a stethoscope around her neck. Tears stream down Mom's cheeks. Kerri stands back. I was right; her eyes are dry. She's cold. I don't know why I'm bawling. Savage never really liked me or Jo that much; he was Mom's cat.

No, that's not true. He was our cat. Mine and Mom's and Jo's. We loved him. We all did.

I bury my head in my knees while Jo says stuff like, "He's in heaven now. He's happy now."

"Nick?" Kerri looms at the side of my chair. "We're going." She lowers herself to the armrest and adds, "Are you okay?" Her hand weights down my head.

I stand up fast. "I have to go," I tell Jo. "I'll call you later." I flip my cell shut.

Swiping my eyes on my arm, I brush by Kerri and head off to find Mom. She's outside at the curb. Empty-handed.

"Where's Savage?" I say.

Mom engulfs me in a hug. She's crying so hard I almost lose it again.

"Where is he?"

Mom inhales a stuttered breath. "He's gone, honey."

"I *know* that. Where is he?" I slip out of her arms.

She glances over my shoulder to the door, where Kerri is emerging from the clinic. Also empty-handed.

"Where. Is. Savage?" I speak the words distinctly so they can't be misunderstood. So Mom can't ignore me.

She looks to Kerri. Kerri answers, "The vet clinic takes care of everything. They dispose of animal bodies."

"No!" I shout. "That's not how we do it." My stomach clenches. "Tell her, Mom."

Mom says . . . nothing.

"Mom!" I yell right in her face. "We have to bury Savage. We saved a place, remember?" Next to Lucky 2 and my Kuhli loach. Alongside all my fish. A place of honor and respect.

Mom runs a hand down the length of my arm.

I jerk away. "Go get him," I order Kerri.

"Nick, I —"

"Get. Him."

Kerri casts Mom this helpless what-do-I-do? look. Mom touches my shoulder. "We can't," she says. "It's illegal. There's a new law that animal bodies have to be disposed of by a licensed removal company. People aren't supposed to bury their pets anymore. I'm sorry, honey."

Illegal? How can it be illegal to keep your family together?

I panic. I can't help but wonder what's going to happen to Savage. Will they just throw him in a Dumpster and bag him with the trash? Will they crush him, or incinerate his body? They'll shovel his ashes out of an oven, then what?

"This is your fault." I point at Kerri. My finger shakes. "If we didn't bring him here he could've died at home and we could've buried him. No one would've known. That's how we do it."

Kerri throws up her hands. "Yeah, it's all my fault. Everything is my fault." Her eyes swell and she storms past us to her car.

Faker.

Unexpectedly, Mom spins me around to face her. "What a horrible thing to say. Go apologize." She shoves me toward Kerri.

I stumble off the curb and fall to my knees. Mom is racing for Kerri, so I scrabble to my feet and dust off my pants, my hands. Then I turn and march toward Mom's car. Never, I think. I'll never forgive her.

Jo

I bounce up onto the truck seat and slam the door. "We've got to stop meeting like this," Jo says. L-3 slobbers all over my face. "Does Erin know you're here?"

It's Erin now. Never Mom.

"I called her." I don't add, She was in a deposition or something and couldn't come to the phone. I didn't leave a message. Hey, I checked in. I'm the dutiful son.

Jo steers out of the Conoco parking lot, and we rattle away. It sounds like the muffler is loose, or the exhaust pipe. Beatrice is rusty and decrepit. Filthy too, like Jo's been four-wheeling her — without me. She says, "You're sneaking out, aren't you?"

I don't answer. I hug L-3. I love this dog. This mental mutt. We can't have any pets now because Kerri is allergic. Yeah, well, what about me? I'm allergic to her.

All I have are my fish. And L-3. I like my fish, but you can't cuddle fish at night. You can't confide in them how much you wish you could be six again. Or eight. How you miss playing Fetch the Football with your three-legged dog, or building snow forts with your mom, or scheming to get your other mom with an artillery of snowballs when she comes home from school.

"What's going on in that scary brain of yours?" Jo reaches over and clamps a claw over my skull. She twists my head on my neck so I'm facing her.

"You don't want to know," I say.

"Actually, I do."

I shrug. "Nothing. Everything. I hate it there. I hate *her*."

Jo's eyes go black. "Has she moved in?"

I shift my thinking. Kerri wasn't the one I meant. "No."

Jo doesn't admonish me anymore about hating people. She hates Kerri; I know she does. Some people deserve it. Jo releases my head.

"I gotta go see a guy about a job, then I thought we'd head up to Bear Lake."

I already know the answer, but I ask anyway, "Did you get fired from FedEx?"

Jo huffs. "No I didn't get fired. And thank you for your confidence in my stability and reliability. I got laid off. There's a difference."

I look at Jo. Really see her. She's thinner than usual. Harder around the edges. Strands of gray filter through her hair. She doesn't wear makeup and her skin looks blotchy.

She still has her dragon tattoo, but the colors are fading, the scales and wings bleeding into her skin. She must sense me studying her because her shoulder twitches, then her right eye, then she screws up her face like the Hunchback. I laugh. I'm going to cook Jo dinner for a week and put it in her freezer. She needs to eat better, healthier. She needs more variety than pizza and hamburgers.

We cruise the warehouse district downtown along factory row. We stop in front of a cinderblock building. There's steam rising from metal grates and a smokestack emitting smelly soot. I don't like it here. It's ghetto. Jo says, "I'll only be a minute. You guys hold down the fort."

I curl an arm around L-3's neck. Jo hops out and hustles toward the building, her hands jamming into her pockets. My nose puckers and my stomach churns.

L-3 gets restless and clambers to the back of the cab, behind our seats. He roots out a squeaky dog toy. There's so much crap back there — fast-food cartons and dirty laundry and gum wrappers, rags and empty quarts of oil. I dig through the rubble and retrieve a sock. A red crew. I sniff it. Clean. She must've run a load of wash to the Laundromat and forgotten to take it upstairs. I wad the sock and shove it into the front pocket of my baggy shorts. If she ever sorts socks, she might wonder why she's missing so many. Chances are that won't happen soon. Anyway, I need them for my collection.

Jo's door flies open and she blows in. Lucky wraps his paws around her neck from the rear, but Jo pushes him away.

I don't like the look on her face. "Didn't you get it?" I ask.

She glares. "Thank you again for your belief and faith in me."

I click my tongue. "What happened?"

The fire in her eyes extinguishes. "What would you think of me hacking slaughter for a living?"

I frown. "What's that?"

She smiles grimly. "Meatpacking."

It triggers the recognizable stench in the air. One time I left hamburger to thaw in the oven so Lucky 2 wouldn't snitch it off the counter. A week went by before I remembered it was in there. We couldn't figure out what smelled so bad. Mom screamed when she found it. The meat was rancid and rotten and there were maggots crawling all over it.

I shudder at the memory.

Jo cranks over the ignition. "What the hell. It pays the rent."

"Is that the only job you can find?" I ask.

"Well, Donald Trump was looking for an apprentice, but apparently he wasn't impressed by my extensive resume. I doubt he even got to page eight, where I lie about graduating from high school."

She runs a red light, and we whack a speed bump. "It's the only job I can find that isn't union. I hate unions. And I need a full-time night shift."

"Why?"

Her eyes cut to me. "For Einstein, you're pretty slow on the uptake."

Oh. She's keeping her days free. For me.

Mom comes tearing out the front door as I'm slogging up the block. "Where have you been?" she screeches.

I stop dead. This is why I asked Jo to drop me at the corner. Mom looks like a pit bull in heat. She comes at me like she's rabid, foaming at the mouth. As strong as my instinct is to flee, I stand my ground. She clenches my shoulders and shakes me. "Where have you been?" Her fury is palpable. "I have the cops out looking for you."

"Huh?" What time is it? I wonder. The sun's going down and the streetlights are flickering on. If my arms weren't pinned to my sides, I'd check my watch. Jo and L-3 and I were having such a blast I guess we lost track of time. Bear Lake's a long drive.

"Where *were* you?" Mom jostles me again.

"Quit it." I push away from her. Kerri exits the front door, punching numbers on her cell.

"Nick!" Mom screams in my face. "Answer me."

"What? I was with Jo."

Mom's eyes raze the landscape and ignite a grass fire. She snaps her head around and seethes at Kerri, "He was with Jo." She scorches me again. "I thought I forbid you to see her."

"You did not." My skin swells.

We have an intense stare down. "You never did," I say. You better not.

Kerri calls, "I let the police know he's home. I left a message." She winces at me like, deep shit, boy.

Mom's still clenching my arms and it's starting to cut off the circulation. I twist out of her grasp. She says, "Where did you go? Why didn't you answer your phone?"

My phone. Where is my phone? I dig in my pocket and feel only Jo's sock. My head spins around. I must've left my phone in Beatrice. I guess I forgot to check messages when we got done fishing. Then after, I forced Jo to stop for groceries so I could cook for her tomorrow.

"You're not going to see her anymore. You're not to talk to her or have any contact whatsoever." Mom sticks out her hand. "Give me your cell. I can't believe she had the gall to come here and pick you up."

My mind is reeling. "She didn't. She doesn't. I mean, I go to her." What does she mean, I can't see her? She can't do this. Forbid me to see Jo?

Mom stiffens her palm. "Give it to me."

My eyes scatter, my brain. "I don't have it. Jo does."

Mom drops her arm. I don't know who she's talking to when she goes, "Now she's stealing from me. That phone doesn't belong to her. If she starts running up charges —"

"She won't. I forgot it, okay? I'll get it back. God."

Mom lets off a puff of steam, then stomps back toward the house.

"You can't do this," I say at her back. Then louder, "You can't do this!"

Mom whirls. "Oh yes, I can. I'll get a restraining order if I have to, but she's not coming anywhere near you again."

Kerri says calmly, "Erin, you don't mean that . . ."

Fear and rage fuel my feet and I charge at Mom, fists

clenched. I bear down on her, flailing at her. She staggers forward and almost falls. Kerri catches her.

"Nick," Kerri says. "Stop it."

I hit her too. Club her in the chest. She doubles over and squeaks in pain. So what. She has it coming.

The cops pull up then and end the drama. I storm to my room.

An ocean of black consumes me, and I feel myself being sucked into the undertow. I'm gasping and groping. I'm drowning in my rage.

Kerri

I don't help her move. Not one box, not one bag, not one suitcase full of her crap. It's a perpetual flow of furniture and lamps and mirrors, books and bedding. Our house is contaminated now. Infected. I want to call the health department and ask them to condemn it. I would if I had a phone.

Mom passes by my open bedroom door and peers in. I meet her eyes. We've barely spoken since "the incident." I hate her. Jo and Mom had a yard sale when we moved from our old house to this one, after I pummeled Josh Lever on the playground. This feels like instant replay. Except all I gave Kerri was a bruised rib, and we're not moving away.

Our yard sale that day made three hundred dollars. As Jo put it, "One person's trash is the next person's treasure." Mom had told Jo to sell her old stereo and Jo said, "That's not trash. That baby's a classic." Mom said, "You don't use it. Sell it." Jo said, "I keep it around to remind me." "Of what?" Mom asked. Jo said the past. It was the one thing she took with her when she left home at sixteen. Mom told her, "You can't live in the past, Jo. You have to let go." Jo didn't want to sell it, but she gave in.

Eventually, Mom always gets her way. You learn that.

The day of the sale Jo asked me to make a sign. In black Magic Marker, she had me print: "Damaged Beyond Repair." She wore the sign around her neck.

Mom was wrong then, and she's wrong still. You don't have to give up your past to move on. You can't. Your past is the part of you that makes you who you are.

Kerri materializes in my doorway. I cringe a little every time I see her. She walks slow and holds her side. "Hey, Nick. Could you give us a hand with my big-screen TV?"

I roll off the bed and cross the room. I shut the door on her. "Thanks," she calls through the wood. "Same to you."

✳

I wake up in a cold sweat. I'm freezing. My sheet is twisted up in my legs and I'm bound tight. I'm wet. Everything's wet. I wonder, Did I have a wet dream? I must have. I stink. My muscles are tense, sore, like I've been hacking through the jungle to outrun the enemy. I'm hot and cold. Burning up.

My thick head lolls to the side and my saltwater aquarium comes into focus. The water is cloudy, murky. I should check the pH, the temp. My arms and legs are paralyzed. I'm bound.

I close my eyes. My heart pumps gallons and gallons of black, brackish blood, water, fish water, waste. I pump, pump. The roaring waves beat in my ears and eyes. My skin is crawling. I can't scream. My mouth won't open, close, work.

Death, I think. This is it. The realization that I'm dying is not unwelcome.

That scares me more than dying.

Jo, please, I pray into the night. Hear me. Come and get me. Give us back our life.

Mom and Jo

Weeks, months, minutes. I don't know time. I have my earphones on, the pulsing, driving bass, clash of cymbals. A
doorbell intrudes. Muted, distant doorbell chime.

Voices. Vibrations. I unplug one ear.

Mom says, "I told you not to come here."

"I have something for Nick."

Jo! I spring out of bed, my earphones ripping off my
head, and fly to the door. I fling it open. She's here! On the
porch.

Mom's at the screen. "You can give it to me."

I rush out the door and throw my arms around Jo. How
long has it been? A week? A lifetime? Hers and mine. She's
warm and alive. She holds me hard, as hard as I hold her.
We're trembling.

"Let him go," Mom says. "Nick, get in here." She thrusts
an arm out at me.

I lurch away. I won't let go of Jo. She heard me, she came for me.

"Jo," Mom goes. "I'm warning you."

The air crackles with the tension between them. I don't care. All I hear and feel are Jo's heart beating against my face and her hot breath on my hair. Breath of life. Almost imperceptibly, she loosens her hold. I tighten mine. "I came to give Nick his phone back." Her voice is monotone. "That's all."

That's not all. She came to get me.

There's a lull. Then Jo says, "This is bullshit, Erin. You don't own him."

"Neither do you," Mom snipes. "And you have no rights to him. You know that."

"Yeah. You've mentioned it once or twice."

Another presence fills the space, the doorway. I sense her aura. It's Kerri, behind Mom. "Hi, Jo," she says. "What's going on?" She's wearing her apron, her chef's apron from the hotel where she works. Garlic permeates the air. She's always smelling up the house.

"Do you want to come in?" Kerri asks. "Nick hasn't been out of his room for, like, a year. Maybe you can get him to rejoin the human race."

Mom says, "Jo's leaving."

Jo says to Kerri, "I guess I'm leaving." She takes a step back, and I move with her. She presses my forehead with her palm and peers into my face. We talk in that silent way we have. We say it all.

Jo's nose flares, and it isn't from garlic. "You reek. You

need a shower." She lifts a lock of my greasy hair and lets it fall. "There's this new product they invented that I saw on TV. They call it shampoo."

I burrow in to hold her again, but she clamps both hands on my rounded shoulders and applies pressure. "I gotta go, Nick," she says. Her eyes fuse to mine. They scream, Please! Please. Don't forget.

She takes a third step back. With me attached.

Mom reaches out and scruffs my T-shirt. She knows I'll tear away. She hooks an arm around my neck.

Kerri clenches Mom's wrist. I choke, and Mom slackens her grip. We're locked in a chain, Mom, Kerri, me, and Jo. I don't know who breaks the first link, but suddenly Jo's free. She's hurrying down the sidewalk. "'Bye, Jo," Kerri calls. "Um, maybe another time."

Mom hauls me inside, bodily. I suppress the urge to lash out. Jo stalls at the end of the driveway next to Beatrice. She turns around. She wants to say something. She wants to fight for me; I know she does. My heart pounds as she heads back, approaches the house. Near the edge of the porch, she stops and says, "I never thought it'd end this way. You know?"

Mom says all snotty, "Well, it did."

"Just like that. You can wipe out all the years we had? Just erase them from your mind?"

Mom expels a gust of air. "People change. They grow up. They move on."

No, I think. I'm not moving on.

My head tingles in back and I jerk around. Kerri's

touched me. She hitches her chin like, Let's go. Let's leave them alone.

She can move on, I think. She can move out.

"Couldn't we just talk, Erin?" Jo says. "How could that hurt?"

"We've said it all, Jo. It's over."

"Not us." Jo's eyes search through the mesh of screen. "Me and Nick. At least let us talk."

All the need and yearning and desperation I feel for her comes burbling up. I struggle to swallow down the gulping tears. Please, Mom. *Please*.

Mom doesn't hear. She doesn't listen. She shakes her head and shuts the door.

Mom

We stop at the mini-mart for a Red Bull. Kerri can't have any other kind of energy drink. It has to be Red Bull.

Mom tries to catch my eye over the seat back. My earphones are on, but only to create white noise. All I want to do is sleep.

She reaches a hand over.

Don't touch me, I think. I struggle to right myself in the backseat. I get about two-thirds of the way up, then my head is too heavy on my neck and I slump over again. I don't know why Mom is dragging me to this stupid competition. Who cares about Kerri? Who cares what she drinks or thinks or does or wants in life? Nobody asks me what I want.

Mom's quick. She yanks off my earphones. "Nick, please. This is an important day for Kerri, and we need to be there for her."

Do we, Mom? Do we need to be there for her?

I don't say it. Even if I could, my lips are numb. My tongue is numb. My face and head and throat — all numb.

"Come on." Mom whaps my knee. "It'll be fun."

Fun.

She smiles somberly. "I know this hasn't been the greatest summer for you."

The speed of the days rivals the sedimentation rate of sewer sludge. I twist my head to gaze out the window. For all I see that registers, or matters, we might as well be moles in an underground labyrinth.

". . . all the change," Mom's voice filters through my brain — also numb. "I'm going to take some time off next month so we can do something together. As a family."

Did she say that? Did she actually say "family"?

Kerri returns, popping the pull tab on her Red Bull. "God, I'm a wreck." She slugs down half the can and refastens her seat belt. "I'm going to crash halfway through this."

"No, you're not." Mom runs an open hand down the back of Kerri's head. "You're going to be great. You're going to kick ass. Right, Nick?" She eyes me over the seat and smiles. There's threat in that smile.

What's she threatening me with? There isn't anything left for you to take from me, Mom.

Kerri swivels her head around and fakes biting her fingernails, like she's all nervous. I bore into Middle Earth.

Kerri takes Mom's hand and fake chews her nails too. Mom laughs. They linger, hands together, as if posing for a wedding photo. Not a picture I'll be adding to my memory book. Mom kisses Kerri then twists on the ignition. A bag of barbecue chips lands in my lap. Kerri says, "Breakfast of champions."

I don't give her the satisfaction. No nod of acknowledgment that it's what I usually eat for breakfast. She's been spying on me. I'm not hungry. Taste buds — numb. Stomach numb.

We get to wherever we're going, and Mom parks. There's a mob of people out on the lawn. Streamers and balloons, tables and chairs. A band or string quartet or something is playing.

Kerri opens another Red Bull and gulps it down. Mom says, "Do you know where you have to go?"

Kerri burps. "To the john to pee. Or throw up."

Mom straightens Kerri's collar and touches her neck. "You'll win. Embrace your inner food critic."

Kerri laughs.

I want to hurl.

Vaguely, I remember why we're here. It's a cooking contest. "Blah, blah top chefs from around the country competing for a spot in an international cook-off."

Whoop de doo.

"It's important to Kerri. Only elite chefs are invited to compete," Mom's words echo.

Whoop de double doo, Mom.

"You're not taking that." Mom snatches the earphones from my numb ears and tosses them back into the car. She remotes the door lock. She and Kerri hold hands and head for the main building, while I lag behind.

It's hot. Humid for July. Too many people milling

around, their talking and laughing absorbed by my brain. I'm already bored. I crave home — house — bed.

"Nick, hurry up." Mom clenches my limp, sweaty hand and yanks my chain. She reels me in close to her and links our arms, smooshing us together. It's weird how our arms are touching and I can feel her cool skin on my hot skin and see her hand clenched around mine, yet I feel as though we're disconnected. Distant. At opposite ends of this campus, this field, this ocean of space. Even at home — house — when we pass from the kitchen to the living room she's gauzy to me. A cloudy film. I used to look at her and see myself reflected, in her eyes, the shape of our ears, the color of our hair. I don't see me anymore. I see Kerri.

"Okay, I'm going to set up and go over my menu again with Gayle and Paul. God, Nick. I wish you were my sous chef today." Kerri fakes a pout.

Yeah, I'd have been real happy to help. Thicken the soup with arsenic.

Kerri kisses Mom again and rushes off to the kitchens. I watch her go. I wonder, Do I want her dead?

No. Just gone.

Mom says, "Let's find out where she'll be stationed and get a good seat."

Whatever.

When we sit, Mom turns to me and says, "I know all this change is a lot for you to handle. Change is always hard."

I don't answer. I stare ahead.

"Kerri and I want to build a life together. With you, of course. We're going to make a new family, the three of us."

Mom takes my limp hand and pulls it into her lap. "You're the most important thing in the world to me, Nick. I love you. You know that. I need you to be happy." She raises my hand and presses it to her lips.

Need? Did she say need? I twist my head slowly to face her. "What about Jo?"

Mom closes her eyes. She expels a long sigh and drops my hand. I relieve her of it.

I've got news for you, Mom, I want to say. I don't *need* your new version of family. "Why can't I see her?"

"Nick —"

"Why can't I talk to her? Why do you hate her so much?"

Mom frowns. "I don't hate her. I just don't trust her. I'm angry with her for showing up unannounced and never calling. I panic when I don't know where you are. . . ."

Or if I'll ever come home, I finish for her. "I'll call you every hour. I promise to remember."

"I worry when you're with her. What if she's drinking again?"

"She's not."

"Or gets fired."

"She won't."

"Or keeps guns in the house. You know how I feel about guns."

I look at Mom.

She stares ahead now. She purses her lips.

"We won't go shooting," I say. "I'll set the timer on my cell —"

"Shh," Mom goes. "They're starting."

The contest is a maze of white-aproned bodies bustling between counters and appliances, flaming woks, grills. There's a
cacophony of voices, buzzers, blenders, mixers, people hol-
lering and barking instructions. The guy next to Mom strikes
up a conversation with her. He's about her age. He could be
my father.

Yeah right. I can only imagine that concept of family.

I double over and let my arms dangle. My eyelids droop
and I zone.

Depart.

Deport.

Desist.

"Sit up, Nick." Mom jerks on my arm. "Kerri's plating."

Who?

Oh. Her.

Dishes clack and ping and all at once a hush settles over
the audience as the judges taste. They chew and score.

I yawn. "Can I go to the bathroom?" I ask Mom.

"Not now."

"I have to take a dump."

She exhales an irritated breath. "Be quiet about it. And
hurry up."

The men's bathroom is at the end of a telescoping corri-
dor. There are classrooms on either side, all the way down.
This must be a school or something. It is, I remember. A
cooking school. Johnson and Wales. Kerri teaches here
part-time in the mornings. At the john, I take my time. I
really only have to pee. I pause to gaze at myself in the mirror over the sink, but I don't see anyone. No living life form.

On the way back my attention is drawn to an object at the other end of the hall. There are two of them. Pay phones.

Mom discontinued our regular phone service when we got our cells. Even if we still had a phone at home, even if she hadn't confiscated my cell, I was forbidden.

It's a miracle I have money. Prisoners of war don't need money.

I lift the receiver and punch in her number. It rings once and she answers out of breath, like she ran.

"It's me."

"Nicky! Hey." She blows out a breath. "Hey." Her voice sounds funny. High and . . . watery. "How the hell are you, buddy?"

Long lost friends. "Fine." My throat catches. We're more than friends.

She doesn't speak for a minute. Neither do I. We're sharing space, time. "Fine, huh?" she says. "Yeah. Me too."

I want to bawl. I want to press my face to the number pad and bawl. Cradling the phone to one ear, I cover the other to block out the world.

"What are you doing?" Jo asks. "Where are you?"

"Here," I choke it out. Nowhere. "Some stupid cooking contest."

"You're in a cooking contest? Whoa. What are you making? Your famous chicken à la mode?"

I smile on the inside. "I'm not in it. Kerri is."

Jo doesn't reply.

I say, "Come and get me."

"Nick —"

"At the cooking school." I don't know the address. I wasn't paying attention on the drive over. "It's Johnson and Wales. You can look it up —"

The phone rips from my ear and slams down on the metal holder. Mom is in my face. "How dare you?"

"How dare you?" I shout. I cry, "How dare you?" I stumble back from Mom. "I hate you."

Her eyes grow wide and she reaches for me, but I slap her hand away. Tears spring to my eyes and I'm sobbing and gasping for air, screaming inside, How dare you, how dare you, How. Dare. You.

✳

I sprawl across the backseat with my face flat to the cushion. It stinks like rotten foam. Mom doesn't talk to me. Kerri didn't win. She didn't even place. She cries on the way home. I don't feel sorry for her. I can't feel anything beyond this hurt and ache that hacks through the numbness and forces me to feel.

Mom

Mom comes home for lunch on Monday and catches me in the act. "What are you doing?"

I drop the fiery stick and watch it fizzle on the floor. Mom rushes over and switches off the gas burner.

"What are you doing?" she asks again. Her voice is calm, but there's an edge to it.

"Nothing." I eye the evidence on the stove.

Mom follows my gaze. The marshmallows, the open box of toothpicks. Charred sticks and glommed goo all over the burners.

Yeah, Mom. This is how I spend my days. Roasting mini marshmallows.

She looks at me like she doesn't know me. I should introduce myself: Nicholas Nathaniel Thomas Tyler. Boy Genius. Solid Waste King. Carbon-based wastoid. Mom steps back, steps away. "I forgot some papers." She clunks her briefcase atop the table and runs upstairs. My eyes focus on the briefcase, the monogram: EAT. I have an irresistible urge to take a knife and gouge into the leather: ME. Or hack at it until it's shredded. Mom returns and flips open the lid. She shoves her papers inside.

I touch her back.

She flinches and holds her heart. "You startled me."

"Mom," I say. "We need to talk."

She looks at me. Then looks away. "Not now, Nick. I'm right in the middle of this court case and I have to get back to work."

"You always say that."

She frowns. "No, I don't. I just can't do this right now."

She knows I want to talk about Jo.

She lifts her briefcase. "I have to go. We'll discuss it tonight."

"No, we won't," I say. "You never want to talk about Jo."

"You're right," she says sharply. "I'm tired of talking about Jo. I'm sick of you always bringing her up in every conversation. And I'm tired of you moping around here like your life is over." Her cell rings, and she opens her briefcase again. She retrieves the silver bullet. "Oh yeah, hi, Zim. I found the deposition. Sorry. I'm on my way back now. What?"

I stare at her as she's talking. She either sees or senses me and moves away into the living room. I follow. She averts her eyes and finishes her conversation, ". . . petition the court. Worse case scenario, I know." She listens. "I know!" She closes the phone. "Find something to do," she says without looking at me. "Paint your room. Go to the public pool. There's plenty to do around here." She heads out.

"There's nothing to do," I say at her back. She opens the door. I yell, "There's *nothing* for me here. I hate it here."

She whirls around and clubs me. I don't know if she was turning and I was closing in, or if she hit me intentionally. She gasps, and her briefcase falls from her hand. With both hands she clamps onto the sides of my face. "Nick, God." She threads her arms around me and pulls me close. "I'm sorry."

My bones are rubber. I'm useless.

"Oh baby . . ." Her arms squeeze the life out of me. What's left of it. "I'm so sorry," she says in my ear. "I didn't mean to . . ." Her teeth chatter like she's freezing. "Nick. Honey."

She's talking to a zombie, to a mummy, to a corpse. When she finally realizes it, she releases me and backs away. Our eyes meet and hold.

Mom's eyes change from liquid to solid. She bends to retrieve her briefcase and says, "I have to go. I promise we'll talk tonight."

✳

I've got my CD player on with the bass amped up, the balance skewed to the right speaker only. It sends concentrated surges of shock waves through my ear, neck, head. I feel . . . drugged. Separated from reality.

Mom barges in. What happened to privacy prevails? "Nick, for God's sake. Turn that down."

I stretch out a hand and punch off my player.

"Thank you," she says.

I flop over onto my stomach, away from her. Vibrations from the bass continue for a moment, then shock. The shock of silence. I shift my head only enough to watch her. She's looming over my fish tank, where another killifish went belly-up.

Mom's focus scatters. "What happened at lunch today . . ." She swallows hard. "I'm under a lot of pressure at work. We have this trial coming up —

"No." She stops herself. "That's no excuse. I'm sorry. It isn't you. You know I'd never hit you."

Never, Mom? Never?

"I'd never hurt you." Her knees buckle, and she perches on my mattress. Her hand lifts to touch my head, but I cower. I cover my face with my arms. She makes the right decision and moves her hand away.

"I wanted to say I'm sorry. Again. I'm sorry about everything." She stands.

Everything, Mom? Everything?

After she leaves, an hour later, two hours, I'm still wondering, Everything, Mom? Does that include having me?

Kerri

In order for my outsides to match my insides, I dye my clothes black. My shirts, my shorts, my shoes. My jeans and socks. I never go upstairs anymore because it's contaminated by *her*, but I have to for the dye. I know she has black hair dye.

The upstairs is different. The bedroom has new furniture, a rocking chair, and a pink and purple dresser drawer. There's no TV. Kerri's jewelry is all over Mom's dresser, and I think I'll steal it. Then I think I don't want to make human contact with Kerri's personal stuff.

Except her dye. There are night-lights on in the hall and the upstairs bathroom. Translucent clown heads and ice-cream cones. They're on day and night, which is weird. She has night-lights downstairs too. Plastic flowers and rainbow hearts. She always leaves lights on behind her, like she's scared of the bogeyman.

In a cabinet next to the sink I find all this nail polish, every conceivable color. I don't touch it. One's spilled. There are three boxes of Clairol. She must buy in bulk, I think. Jewelry, nail polish, hair dye, night-lights.

I don't have that many clothes. Two washers full. They come out kind of slate gray, but that's okay. I make sure to leave a mess for Kerri to clean up. And the empty dye boxes so she'll know I've violated her space.

✳

Mom doesn't say anything. She barely looks at me. Kerri only says, "If you'd asked, I'd have gotten you some black Rit."

Shut up, I think. Your roots are showing.

Kerri scans me up and down. She nods her head. "Cool," she says. Like she gets it.

Which almost makes me wish I hadn't done it.

Mom

Mom throws back my covers and drags me bodily out of bed to eat breakfast with her and Kerri. They're celebrating their one-month anniversary of living together. I guess they expect me to party with them. Embrace the Family Moment. I can think of things I'd like to do with the candles on the cake. You never know when you're going to need a fire.

"How about California?" Mom says. "We could spend a whole week out there seeing sights and going to the beach. We could either drive or fly. I'd rather fly and rent a car." She's reading the Travel and Leisure section of the Sunday paper. Kerri's got the Sports.

I bet dyed black hair burns fast.

Mom says, "What do you think, Nick? You've always wanted to see the ocean. We could head down the coast, maybe hit Disneyland."

I continue doing what I'm doing — scraping my knuckles with a serrated knife.

Mom sighs. "Nick, are you listening?"

Are you speaking to me?

Kerri pipes up from her chair, which used to be Jo's chair. "That sounds awesome, Erin. I'm glad you're finally taking a vacation. You need it."

I feel Kerri's eyes drilling holes into the base of my skull. What?

Kerri says, "We could go to Sea World in San Diego. They have this awesome shark exhibit."

Shut up, I think. Remove the word "awesome" from your vocabulary.

"Isn't that where the Institution of Oceanography is, Nick?" Mom asks. "That's all you talked about last year, going to Scripps Institution of Oceanography." She says to Kerri, "He wants to be a marine biologist."

No, I don't. In a previous life maybe. I don't remember telling her about Scripps Institute, or my plans for the future. I told Jo. We were talking about going to California once, over spring break. Before the break. The break-up.

"What do you think? Will that resurrect you from the grave?" Mom's speaking to me now, I guess. One set of knuckles is flaky white with serrated skin. I've drawn blood, so I start on the other.

Kerri scoots back her — Jo's — chair. "He didn't hear you," she says. "He's in the dead zone." She grabs the knife out of my hand and glares at me. "What is your problem?"

"You," I say.

Mom's up, clasping my wrist and jamming me against the counter. Do it, I think. Hit me. I dare you.

Her eyes get this wild, frightened look. She eyes the knife. And my bloody knuckles. Her face pales, and she lets me go. With a swish of robe, she sprints up the stairs.

"Good job," Kerri says. "Way to go. I hope you know what you're doing to her."

I cut her a look.

Kerri wets a dishrag under the faucet and before I can retract them, has my hands wrapped up in it. She rubs them roughly. "For weeks now she's been trying to come up with something that'll make you happy. Anything to bring you out of this funk you're in and cheer you up. I don't know why she bothers." Kerri shoves the bloody dishrag at my chest. "Yes, I do. Because she loves you," Kerri adds. "You might try giving some of that back." She storms up the stairs after Mom.

"There's only one thing that'll make me happy," I say to empty space.

*

I spend the day in my room. Snails crawl. Algae grows. I know I should check the tanks, but I don't have the energy. Or the interest.

I can't stand it anymore. I have to do something. I know what it is. I go out to the living room and find Mom and Kerri there. Mom's reading a paperback, her head in Kerri's lap, and Kerri's knitting, watching her big-screen TV.

I stand in front of them. "I want to live with Jo."

Mom doesn't look up. Kerri does.

"I want Jo to adopt me so I can live with her."

Mom shuts her book and rises, elevates to full height, and passes me without a glance. I trail her to the kitchen. She opens the fridge and removes a carton of yogurt.

"Mom." I touch her shoulder. "I want to live with Jo."

She wheels around. "Who gave you that idea?"

What? "Me," I say.

Mom goes, "Are you talking to her? Are you seeing her? You've been sneaking out to be with her, haven't you?"

I shake my head. "No."

Mom focuses on me, hard, like she's trying to excavate the truth. It's the truth, Mom. Believe it.

"We haven't talked," I say out loud. "I haven't seen Jo." I've respected your wishes. I've respected you, your position, your power over me. I've kept my vow to honor you.

Respect me. Honor me. "I want to live with Jo," I repeat. "I know it'll be all right with her."

Mom pushes past me.

"It's what I want, Mom. It's what'll make me happy."

"Living with Jo isn't going to make you happy. I can tell you that."

"Just because it didn't work out for you doesn't mean it won't for me."

There's a long moment of silence. I say again, "This is what I want, Mom."

"I don't care what you want," she snaps. "This is what you get. This is the way it is, Nick. Get used to it."

"No," I say. "I want to live with Jo."

"Well, you can't!" She slams the yogurt down on the table and the contents explode. Forget the glops of pink and white everywhere, I think she hurt her wrist. She's whimpering and clutching it to her chest, her eyes filling with tears. Kerri runs in. "What'd he do? Did he hurt you? Are you okay?" Mom raises her chin and blinks at me. "It's never going to happen, Nick," she says. "Get it out of your head."

✳

I can't get it out of my head. My angelfish, the one I named Sasha, has been listless all week. I don't even care. I can't watch the inevitable and know the part I've played in it. I camp out on the bottom stair in the laundry room. I lay there all night, stiff and cold. At dawn, Mom opens her door and, slipping an arm through the sleeve of her suit jacket, whispers into the room, "Sorry if I woke you, sweetheart. Go back to sleep."

I ambush her halfway up the stairs. "Mom. I want to live with Jo."

Mom slows her descent momentarily and grits her teeth. She moves again, wedging by me, and continues to the landing, through the laundry room and into the kitchen. I follow her. The coffeemaker, set on automatic, gurgles the end of the brew cycle, and Mom pours herself a steaming cup.

"I want —"

"Stop it, Nick."

"I want to live —"

"Stop!"

The clomp on the stairs behind us makes us both turn.

Kerri enters, yawning.

I tell Kerri, "I want to live with Jo."

She holds my eyes. She acts like she wants to say something, then changes her mind, I guess. Kerri will let me go. She hates me. She'd do anything to get rid of me so she can have Mom all to herself.

I resume with Mom, "I want to live —"

"Shut up, Nick. Just shut up!"

"Erin," Kerri's voice rises.

"What!" Mom snaps at her.

Kerri flinches. Pushing her hair off her face with both hands, she says, "At least let him talk to her."

Mom's eyes shoot fireballs. "Stay out of it. This is none of your business."

Kerri reels. "Well, excuse me for caring." She plucks her chef's jacket off a hanger in the laundry room and crashes out the back door. She's barefoot and has on a flimsy nightshirt.

"I want to live with Jo."

Mom sets her coffee cup down hard in the sink. Drops of hot coffee singe my arm. She wrenches her briefcase off the table and stalks out the door.

✳

My door opens. Mom flicks on my overhead light and blinds me. "I know you're not asleep," she says. "I want to talk to you."

Her eyes skitter around the room and locate my desk chair. It's shoved against the wall. She wheels it over, carts it across the floating debris from the shipwreck on my floor, and clears the seat. The stuff on it is mostly Jo's socks. Her white and red crews. Her wool sock with the hole in the toe. Mom sits.

"I hate it here, Mom," I tell her.

"Nick —"

"I don't hate you," I add quickly. "I didn't mean to say that." Before. The other time. She understands about impulses, right? She didn't mean to hit me. "I just don't want to be here. I want to live with Jo." I don't add, It's not that I don't need you. I need you to give me what I want.

"Look," she says. "I know you're not crazy about Kerri, but if you'd give her a chance —"

"No." I shake my head. "That's not it. It's not Kerri. It's . . . this." It takes tremendous energy to raise my arm. I wave it once across my body. I'm not sure what "this" encompasses. This place. This life. This . . . person.

Mom presses her fingers to her forehead like she has a headache. "Okay, I understand. It's the memories in this house. I'm sorry, honey. Naturally, you have all these bad associations."

"No." My head shakes again. It's hard to move, to engage so many muscles at once.

"It's not a problem." Mom lowers her hand to her lap, laces her fingers together, and smiles. "I don't have any real attachment to this place. It's close to your school, but there are lots of other houses in the area. In fact, Kerri and I have been talking about moving closer to my office, maybe building a house together —"

"No," I cut her off. "It's not the house. It's . . ." My hand flattens on my chest. "Me." I thump it once. "Me." I thump again. Then, rhythmically, "I" — thump — "hate" — thump — "me." My arm is so heavy.

"Nicky." Mom gets up off the chair and moves to the bed. She sits down beside me. "Honey," she says softly. "You don't mean that." She takes my dead hand and examines the scabs.

"Please, Mom," I beg her. "Let me live with Jo."

Mom presses my hand lightly between hers. Her voice is even when she says, "Try to understand. I'm your mother, your biological mother. Parents and their children are meant to be together. We have a bond. We're family. We're part of each other and we need to stay together. I love you. You're my son." She swallows once. "Besides, I have legal custody of you. It would never work because Jo never adopted you. Which, apparently, you know."

"Why didn't she?" I ask. I already know the answer.

Mom's eyes close. She knows the answer too. I fill her in, in case she's forgotten. "Because you decided it wasn't necessary. You and Jo got married. Not legally, of course. But you made a vow to always be together. You trusted each other. You went on faith."

"God," Mom expels the word. "I can't believe she tells you these things."

"And Jo promised you on the day I was born that she would love me like I was her own. Because she loved you.

She promised me — you *both* promised — that we would always be together."

Mom barks, "Well it didn't work out that way, okay? People change. They grow up. They grow apart."

"Not from me," I tell her.

Mom's eyes well with tears and she pushes to her feet.

There's more I have to say. It's time. There's too much left unsaid between us, too many unspoken fears. "When you had your cancer, Jo got really scared and wanted to adopt me then. But she didn't want you to believe for a minute, not for one minute, Mom, that you might die."

"Stop it." Mom's searching frantically for something. A tissue? The only thing she can find is a bloody T-shirt — the one I wore when I carved the dragon on my arm. Or tried to.

My mouth's dry. I'm shaking. I haven't spoken this way to Mom — ever.

She doesn't seem to notice the blood. There are so many things she doesn't notice. Swiping at her snot, she says, "I know you think Jo needs you, and you feel sorry for her because she's all alone. That's nobody's fault but her own." Mom blows her nose and wads up the T-shirt. "She could've reconciled with her parents, but she didn't. She has two half brothers in Texas she never talks to, and cousins and aunts and uncles. She has family everywhere. Even if she didn't, she could've been part of my family — *our* family. She never even tried to get along with Neenee and Poppa."

"No," I say. Mom isn't listening — still.

"She's irresponsible. She can't hold down a job. She can't take care of anything by herself."

"She takes care of me."

That quiets Mom — for an instant. "I never neglected you. Never."

Now I close my eyes. "Mom." She's dense. "You're my birth mom. I know that. I *get* that." I open my eyes. "But Jo . . ." I hesitate because I don't know how Mom's going to react to this. She has to know, though. Deep in her heart I think she does, and that's the problem. That's what makes it so hard to say. "Jo's my real mom."

There, the truth is out. It's been eating at me for a while. Since Jo left. The most important person in my life has been taken from me. It's like she died, only worse. Because it isn't death that's keeping us apart. It's life.

Kerri

Pans clang. Cupboards slam. Voices clash in battle. It's war.
The house is a battle zone.

Like the old days — with one difference. Mom's the one
yelling. Mom's on the offensive.

Then, silence. Profound silence. The house settling. My
consciousness lifting, billowing me away.

I bolt awake. Another day, or night, has passed.

Three days, I think it's been. For three days Mom and
Kerri haven't spoken to each other. They don't speak to me
either, which is fine. Why waste words?

I like the yelling better, the slamming of doors. The silent
treatment creeps me out. It always has.

Maybe now she'll go. She can leave the big-screen TV,
since it's all I have to do all day. I'm out of marshmallows
and hair dye. Mom removed the knives from the silverware

drawer. She doesn't realize how many other kinds of weapons there are.

I get up once in the middle of the night to raid the refrigerator. Kerri always brings leftovers home from the hotel, stacks of Styrofoam cartons, which I work my way through. There's weird stuff like gnocci and black bean patties. Sweet and sour ribs. I plan to eat her out of house and home, literally.

Then I see her out back on the porch stoop, hunched over. She must sense me looking because she turns. We stare at each other. There's an incoming message from her to me, but I don't receive it. I shut down the communication station and return to my molehole.

In the morning Kerri tries to engage me in conversation. "Sleepwalker," she says. "We're out of chips for breakfast, but you can bagel it. I'm trying these funky combos like raisin and tomato. Blueberry basil." She sticks out a fleshy tongue, then extends a plate with five or six bagels. "See if they make you hurl."

When I don't jump at her offer, she sets the plate back on the table. "I'll bring something home from work for your midnight snack. What do you want?"

Is that a question? Does she really need me to answer? She knows what I want.

She says, "This is fun, isn't it? Fun and games with family dynamics."

Mom sweeps down the stairs in her power suit and pours a cup of coffee.

"Good morning," Kerri says to her.

Mom's eyes are swollen.

Kerri adds, "Would you like me to make you an omelet?"

Mom looks at her. They look at each other. I'm caught in the tidal wave of emotion that passes between them. They heave toward each other and lock in an embrace.

Casually, deliberately, I push a glass off the counter. It falls to the floor, but doesn't shatter. It rolls near Mom's foot.

She has to detach from Kerri to pick it up. She sets it in the sink and, averting her eyes from both of us, murmurs, "Thanks. I'm not hungry." Her gaze hovers over the plate on the table. "Oh . . . maybe a bagel."

That makes Kerri smile. Mom grabs a blueberry one and bites into it. "Mmm." Her eyes pop. "Yum. This is delicious." She and Kerri have another Magic Moment. They apologize. They kiss. They'll talk later. Then Mom takes off, briefcase in tow.

Kerri hangs her head. "God. I don't know what I'm supposed to do."

Leave, I almost say. Set your hair on fire.

"I want to help you, Nick," she says. "More than anything, I want to make this right. I just don't know how."

I almost say, Any idiot could figure it out.

I hear them upstairs. The bedroom door is ajar and they're talking. Not loud. It's late, after midnight, and I'm prowling around the house. I am a sleepwalker. Pathological liar that she is, Kerri didn't bring home any new food. There are a dozen cans of Red Bull in the refrigerator and the same take-out cartons as yesterday. I'm starving. Out of habit, I open the back cupboard behind the stove. Someone replenished my stock of potato chips.

"No," I hear upstairs. "He's not old enough to know what he wants."

"Erin. He is. I know you're afraid. . . ."

Their voices garble. ". . . not what you think."

I creep up the stairs with sharklike stealth. I want to know Mom's fears. The night-light is on in the hallway between their bedroom and bathroom. Kerri's afraid of the dark. That's her bogeyman.

I move in as close as possible, right outside the door. I tread soundlessly. Inside their bedroom I note shapes: Squares and rectangles, a CD player and a mirror I haven't seen before. They're in bed, two lumpy shapes under the top sheet. Kerri's on her side, propped on her elbow, facing Mom. My eyes follow her bumpy backbone all the way down from her neck to the bottom of her spine. She's only halfway covered.

"I want him to have a family like I did," Mom says. "I have such happy childhood memories."

Kerri goes, "Erin, think about that. He's never going to have the so-called traditional family. Believe me, they're not all idyllic. Yours was an exception."

Mom sighs. "I know. I just wonder sometimes what it's done to him."

"He seems pretty normal to me. You should've seen me at thirteen. Talk about dark and moody."

"I wanted to have it all," Mom continues, like she's talking out loud to herself. "I didn't want to believe my sexuality was limiting, that I'd never have a family because I was a lesbian. I wonder, though, if it was selfish."

Kerri runs her fingertips down Mom's arm. "You're a great mom. Nick's just going through a traumatic time right now."

Mom says, "I wonder if he'd be better off . . ." She stops.

My heart pounds. Say it, Mom. Say it. With Jo.

Kerri ventures, "Not being born?"

What? No. Mom doesn't confirm or deny. My stomach roils.

"Don't even think that, Erin. I'm sure that hasn't even crossed his mind."

In a small voice, Mom says, "I'm not so sure."

Kerri goes, "Ask him."

Mom stares up at the ceiling. Kerri watches her. I hold my breath.

"The thing is . . ." Kerri hesitates. She takes a deep breath. "The thing is, when he's unhappy, you're unhappy. When you're unhappy, I'm unhappy. It's this cycle of misery we're perpetuating. You know?" She winds a lank of white hair behind her ear and it falls back over her face. "There's bad karma in this house, Erin. I hate it."

Mom whispers, "I know."

Kerri caresses Mom's face. "We'll get through it. We will. You're my everything, you know. I'd do whatever you need to make you happy. To make us all happy."

Mom's chest rises and falls. "Just don't make me choose," she says.

Kerri's back goes stiff. "I'm not. I would never —"

"Because you know who'd win."

Kerri swings out a leg and straggles off the edge of the bed. "I didn't think it was a contest." She's charging at me, and I scramble. I jump to my feet and bound down the stairs. On the landing, I glance back up and see her, silhouetted in the light, scowling at me.

I slither back to my room. I don't feel so good.

✳

She raps softly on my door. "Nick," she whisper-calls. "Are you awake?"

It's morning. Sunlight seeps in around my window shades, even though I keep them pulled down. I like the dark. I'm a denizen of the dark.

"Sleepwalker?"

I don't move. What if I open my door and she's standing there naked? I don't know if she was earlier or not. All I really saw was a bunch of skin and hair.

I hold my breath, wait until I sense she's gone, then get up and go to the bathroom. On my way back I detect a foreign object in my room. I skim lightly across the ocean bottom to investigate.

It's a note. I unfold it. A penciled message reads: "Earth to Nick." There's a drawing of a spaceship. On the side panel it says, MOTHERSHIP.

Not even funny.

There's a second sheet of steno paper on the floor. I pick

it up. "Come to work with me today." The door on the ship is open, and two eyeballs peer out.

Why would I go to work with her? As she's ripping out a third sheet to slide under the door, I open the door.

Kerri springs back. "God. You scared me."

I retrieve the note from the floor. It's a sketch of me, two of me, actually. One with a frowny face. One all smiley. Not bad caricatures. I didn't know she could draw.

"Nick," she says. "I really want you to come to work with me today. I need your help on something."

I just look at her.

"Please?" She falls to her knees and steeples her hands. "Pleeease? Pretty please? I promise, I'll make it worth your while."

She's insane. I don't remember the last time anyone said please to me. Everyone does whatever they want with me, or to me.

I think about it. I have to admit I'm curious. What does she need me for? Plus, I'm dying to get out of this house.

What else is there to do? "Whatever."

✳

As we're driving away from the house, I'm wishing I never had to come back here. As soon as Kerri starts work and forgets me, I'm running. I'm taking off and never looking back.

"Here." Kerri hands me something. "Call her." It's her cell.

I must look stupid, because she angles her head like, Hello? "Call Jo and tell her to meet us at Johnson and Wales. Ask her if she can. If she needs directions . . ."

My whole body is swelling. My heart is pulsing. I can't believe it. I punch in the numbers and she answers on the first ring.

"Jo."

"Nicky!" The sound of her voice is a bass riff.

"Yeah."

"Hey. Buddy."

"Hey." Hey Jo. I curl in on myself and feel the heat circulating through my veins. A lightness of being lifts me.

"Whassup?" she says. "Where are you?"

I tell her, "In the car. Can you come and get me?" I tell her where to pick me up. Johnson and Wales. "That cooking school."

She hesitates. "Today? Now?" Then says, "Sure. Yeah, of course."

Kerri's fingers wiggle in my face. "Let me talk to her."

I don't want to. I don't want to lose our connection. We're crossing a busy intersection and Kerri's merging, checking over her shoulder, her stubby fingers and painted nails almost touching me. I plop the phone in her hand.

"Jo," Kerri goes. "It's Kerri. I know this is unexpected. Is today good for you?" She listens. She frowns. "Oh God. I'm sorry."

My ears roar.

Kerri says, "We could do it tomorrow." She brakes at a

light, squealing to a stop. She switches the phone to her other ear and adds, "Okay. If you're sure." She listens. "Are you kidding?" Kerri lets out a short laugh. "When she finds out, we'll be dog meat. Let me rephrase that. *I'll* be dog meat."

They're talking about Mom, I know.

Kerri says, "No. I have to tell her. Don't worry. I'll take the heat." Kerri winks at me. The light changes, and she switches ears again. I want to talk to Jo. Kerri rattles off directions, then flips the phone closed.

"Hey, I wasn't done!"

"She'll meet us at ten."

My joy spikes. "What time is it?" I ask. I quit wearing a watch when time sludged to a stop.

Kerri answers, "Quarter to nine." She gazes out the side window at all the trees whizzing by, the strip malls and factories. She adds under her breath, "This better be worth it."

I say, "Someone has to break the cycle of misery."

Kerri whips around and drops a jaw.

I almost laugh.

✷

I'm not expecting Jo to arrive in a cab. "Beatrice finally bit it," she says. We've hugged and choked back tears, and now we're heading out across the lawn, the campus. I feel mad. Happy and mad. I should've been there when the towing company came to haul away Beatrice. I would've liked a few minutes to sit in her and remember. Imprint the sights and smells of her, the feel of the vinyl seat cover on my bare legs. I might've pried off a radio knob to keep as a souvenir.

Jo says, "Didn't that shirt used to be yellow?"

I don't explain. Instead I ask, "Where's Lucky?"

Jo lets out this audible sigh of pain. "He's gone. I had to give him up. He barked all night and the neighbors complained. Plus, he ate half the front door."

I grimace.

"Yeah. Separation anxiety. You know?"

Do I ever. I slide my arm around Jo's back and rest my head against her shoulder. "We'll get a cat," I say.

"Right. Or a rat. Hey, how about fish? I've always had a thing for fish."

I grin. I don't tell her about my fish. It wouldn't make her happy, and I don't want to break the cycle of happiness.

✳

It's the best day of my life. Kerri leaves us alone. Jo and I just hang out and talk. My throat gets sore from all the talking. We spar a while on the lawn and wrestle; we find an old tennis ball and toss it around.

On the way home I tell Kerri, "Thanks." Sincerely.

She smiles. "You're welcome."

Before we left I told Jo that Kerri would take her home, but Jo insisted on calling a cab. I tell Kerri, "Tomorrow you can just drop me off at Jo's."

Kerri's face changes. She reaches up and scratches her

eyebrow ring. "Uh . . . the thing is . . ." She licks her upper lip. "There's no tomorrow, Nick. I mean, there is, but this was a one-time deal. You know? I thought it'd help you to see her. I know how much you miss Jo. But this doesn't change anything. You know your mom will never change her mind. She'll never let you —" Kerri stops. "Jo understood that. Right?"

No. If she did, she didn't convey her understanding to me. I say, "Don't tell Mom."

Kerri clicks her tongue. "I have to tell her. I'm not going to lie to her."

"You already did."

Kerri's face flushes. "Okay. But it's more like I'm delaying the truth. I'm going to tell her." We pull up in front of the house and this overwhelming sense of dread descends from the sky. It envelopes me.

"She doesn't have to know," I say. "It'll make her unhappy. I won't tell her, I promise."

"Ni-ick." Kerri pouts. "I can't do that. Our relationship is based on trust. I just thought it'd cheer you up to see Jo. I thought . . ." Her tongue catches on the roof of her mouth and her voice trails off. She looks at me, hard. I hope she sees what she's just done to me. "Oh." Her shoulders slump. Her voice breaks and she goes, "Oh, Nick. I'm . . . sorry."

✳

Sorry. Sorry, sorry, sorry. The word to live by in our house. Kerri's as good as her word. She told Mom and Mom ripped into me. ME. She grounded me for the rest of the summer. So much for taking the heat, Kerri. So much for sorry. That's what trust will get you. Delaying the truth only buys a prolonged cycle of silence and misery. For reminding me what I could never have, for giving it to me then taking it away, I hate Kerri now with all my heart.

Mom

Mom comes into my room with my laundry. I don't even care that she didn't knock. I have nothing to hide.

I have nothing.

Mom sets a stack of clothes on my bed and says, "You'll want to start clearing out some of your old stuff and deciding what to pack. You know the house is going up for sale tomorrow and if it sells right away, we —" The air's suddenly stagnant.

I roll my head and look at her. Mom's staring at my saltwater tank.

She says, "What did you do?"

I follow her eyes. I focus on nothing. "I unplugged them."

Her eyes dart around the room, to all the tanks. "What'd you do with the fish?"

At first I don't answer. Then I say, "Nothing."

"Nothing? You mean you . . ." Gazing at the murky

water, at the silent air pumps and filters, the cold lights and gray algae, she gets it.

I confirm, "I killed them." I bagged them and tossed them out with the trash.

Mom gives me this look, like, horrified, stunned.

Slowly, she backs out of my room. There, I think, she finally knows the truth about me. She sees me for what I am. A monster.

Mom

A flurry of commotion signals change. It's moving day. We're moving.

Mom does a weird thing: She says, "Nick, run down to Ace Hardware and get us more bubble wrap." She hands me a twenty.

I look at her for a moment.

She looks back at me. "Hurry up."

I scoot out the door. Doesn't she know how far a twenty will carry me?

The Ace Hardware is in a strip mall about a quarter mile away. When I arrive, I ask the clerk if I can use the phone. He says, "We don't have a phone." He's lying. He means the phone isn't available to a punk like me. I hope he steps on a rake.

I start walking to Jo's. It's way too far to walk. Without thinking, I change direction and head toward the dump.

The city landfill where we took a bunch of trash the other day. It's crazy, I know, but I need to find my fish. They're decomposed by now, but I never should have thrown them into the trash like they were garbage. They weren't garbage. They were alive and beautiful, and they depended on me to keep them that way. I loved those fish. I may be a murderer, but they didn't ask to be born. They weren't given a choice about who would raise them, feed and nurture them, keep them safe. I let them down. They depended on me and I failed them. The least I can do is give them a proper burial.

I don't find my fish where we threw our trash. There aren't any blue plastic bags. The only thing I find in the dump is filthy stinking rot.

My fish hate me.

Stupid, I think. Fish don't hate. Except . . . they do. I know they feel. They feel pain and love and loss.

It begins to rain. Hard. Now I'm hungry and wet and cold. I feel like a little kid who runs away from home and gets as far as the corner.

The gutters are overflowing with runoff from roofs, and I get a sudden urge to wade. My first step in the water shocks me. It's frigid. A memory floods my brain. It's summer and I'm a little kid, wading up the street in the gutter. The water splashes over my toes and feet and ankles. Mom and Jo are sitting on the porch, watching me. They're drinking beer and laughing.

They're laughing. Wow. That was a long time ago. Back when they could still laugh together. When the water was warm and comforting, not freezing like this.

I don't consciously head in any direction, but all at once the house comes into view. The FOR SALE sign. A truck parked in the open garage.

I slow. I don't know that truck. It's a black Chevy Avalanche. For some reason, I slog faster. I jump up onto the sidewalk to hurry, to sprint the rest of the way.

Then I see her.

She's lugging a couple of boxes out the front door. She smiles when our eyes meet, and dumps the boxes into the truck bed. I fly to her. My feet are fins. Jo's smile fades. "Where the hell have you been?" she snarls. "Your mom said she sent you on an errand over an hour ago. She's ready to call out the National Guard. What kind of shit is that?" Jo raises my chin with her fist. She scans me up and down, then hugs me. She holds me hard. I melt.

Clenching my upper arms, she thrusts me away. "You're soaked. And filthy. Look at your pants and shoes."

I'm gasping for air from the running, the adrenaline rush of seeing her. I glance down, but my eyes don't focus. My glasses are fogged. "I went fishing," I say. My fingernails are jagged and crusted with dirt.

"Yeah, right." She smacks my head. "What did you catch, pneumonia?" Her hand lingers on my head. My vision clears.

At her expression, my stomach plunges. Not that look. Not . . . longing. I fling my arms around her and lock my hands in back. I am *not*. Letting *go*.

She smashes my head against her chest.

I manage to verbalize one thing: "We're moving."

"Yeah, your mom told me." She must sense my throat constricting, or hear it in my voice. She holds me back and frowns. "Didn't she tell you?"

"What?"

Jo rolls her eyes. "Come on." She clamps a metal claw over my head and cranks my skull around. She steers me toward the house. "He's back," she calls inside. "You guys didn't move fast enough."

A speedboat roars through my brain. We're moving. We're moving on. I can't stop the motion.

My squishy sneakers drown out the roar. Jo's beside me. She's behind me. I keep looking back. She's with me, in the house, the hall. In my room. Mom's duct-taping the lid on my saltwater aquarium. Why? Even the coral frags are dead now.

She twists her head and sees me. A rush of relief washes over her face.

Jo says, "You didn't tell him."

Mom asks, "Did you get the bubble wrap?"

Damn. I knew there was something. . . .

Mom's eyes widen and she cocks her head.

Sorry, I think.

Jo's says, "Erin, why didn't you tell Nick?"

Mom resumes her task. She rips off a hunk of tape and goes, "I wanted it to be a surprise."

What are they talking about? The fact that they're talking at all makes me feel like I missed something. How long have I been gone?

"I assume you want to take all your tanks," Mom says.

Is that a question? I don't know the answer.

She adds, "Jo says there's no room for your furniture, so we'll take it with us."

What? I look from Mom to Jo. *What?* Jo starts emptying my dresser drawers into a trash bag. "Tell him," Jo says to Mom.

Mom presses her lips together. She says, "You'll come and visit occasionally. I hope."

"Erin, for God's sake." Jo scoffs at her. "You're only moving across town. You make it sound like I'm taking him to Uranus." She smirks at me. "Up Uranus."

Mom lowers her head.

Jo adds, "You'll see him all the time. We'll work out a schedule."

I feel like I'm watching a movie — the movie of my life. I should make an entrance here somewhere. My mind is swirling again, clouding. I can't think. Then, like a bolt of lightning, I understand. Happiness explodes in a kaleidoscope of colors so sharp and intense they're outside the visual spectrum.

"Don't just stand there looking like a retard." Jo tosses me an empty box. "Pack up your computer. There's nowhere to plug it in, but I guess that's not a problem since the electricity's off. Maybe we can pawn it for food."

I say, just to be sure I've got it, "I'm moving in with you. Right?"

Jo says to Mom, "We should've specified brain cells when we were picking out sperm."

I can't help myself. I throw my arms around Jo's back. She stumbles forward, but she drops my jocks and yanks me around, smothering me in a fierce embrace. She says, between clenched teeth, "Go tell your mother thank you."

I let Jo go and stagger over to Mom. I want to hug her so bad, but I can't. She's brittle. My eyes search out Jo's. She threatens me with a fist. "Mom?"

Mom jerks around.

I swallow. "I . . ." My lips quiver. "Thank you, Mom." I add, "I love you."

Her eyes well with tears. It looks like she's already been crying. She doesn't say a word, just opens her arms to me.

I fall into them. She feels solid and strong, soft and familiar. I say, "I love both you guys." In different ways, I don't add. For different reasons. But I love you both the same.

Mom smiles at me — a sort of happy, sad smile.

"Why did you keep it a surprise?" I ask. "Why didn't you tell me? When did you decide?"

She goes to answer, but no words come out of her mouth. She starts, "I thought —" She swallows. "I hoped — you might change your mind. Or I could." Her eyes penetrate me.

"Nick," she says, taking my hand into her lap and pulling me down beside her. "I get it now, okay? You belong with Jo. I'm sorry it took so long for me to figure it out, and you've been so miserable. I love you. I only ever wanted you to be happy."

She doesn't say, With me, but I know she's thinking it.

I'm sorry, Mom. I'm sorry.

Her eyes pool again and now mine do, too. If she starts bawling, my floodgates will open.

Mom sniffs and presses a fist under her nostrils. "I shouldn't have kept it a secret. I talked to Jo last week after . . ." Her hand releases mine, and she wipes her nose with the back of her hand. "Your fish."

My fish. Yeah.

She takes a deep breath. "Are you surprised?"

I nod.

"Happy?" she asks.

I don't nod. Because suddenly I don't feel so happy. I never wanted to make her miserable. There's no way to win.

Mom smiles. I snake my arms around her waist and hug her hard. She hugs me back. She's going to say something else, when Jo wrenches open my bottom desk drawer and yells, "What the hell's this?" She bolts upright, clutching a fistful of socks.

Uh-oh.

"These are mine. I wondered where these went."

I exaggerate a grin at her.

"What are you, some kind of pervert? Are you hoarding women's underwear?"

I click my tongue. "It's not underwear."

I think she'd understand, but I'm not about to talk about it now. Not with Mom here.

Jo shakes her head at Mom. "What kind of kid did we raise? A thief and a pervert."

"Don't forget retard," I say.

Mom goes, "Take this out to Jo's truck." She lifts and hands me my aquarium. She gives me a nudge in the direction of the door.

I scurry out with the tank.

While I'm in the garage, I see Kerri's car, loaded to the hilt. There's music coming from the back of the house, so I trail it around to the yard. The rain has stopped, and the air smells sweet and new. I see Kerri standing on the patio, arms folded loosely around herself. She turns her face to the sun and closes her eyes. I take a step forward. Kerri sees or senses me and goes back inside.

The urge to follow her is strong.

In the house I almost trip over her. She's plopped onto the bottom step and hunched over, elbows on knees. When my knee clobbers her head, she raises up fast. "Oh, sorry," I say.

Suddenly I feel this deep, tremendous sorrow and regret for everything that's gone down between us. It wasn't Kerri's fault. I know that.

"So," she says. "Are you going now?"

"You wish." I sink down beside her.

"Nick, I don't want you gone. I never did. If that's what you think —"

"No. I'm kidding." I'm the one who wanted you gone.

She fixes on me, on my face. I notice for the first time how her eyes are different colors. One's turquoise and the other's aquamarine. There's a difference. It's subtle, but I can detect it in fish. Tetras especially. How the play of light and shadow changes their color and luminescence. Fish will change before your very eyes.

"Mom's talking to Jo."

Kerri's penciled eyebrows arch. "A Kodak moment."

"Really," I say. "What happened?"

Because I want to know what made the difference in Mom. What finally got through to her, besides my fish. There had to be more.

Kerri wiggles her bare toes. They're painted all different colors, and she has a toe ring on the left pinkie. "She's worried about what's happening to you." Kerri adds, "What you're becoming. She wanted to send you to a shrink, but I told her she was just avoiding the truth. The truth being, she's the one contributing to your unhappiness. To the whole cycle here."

My jaw unhinges. The truth hurts.

"She knew that. I didn't have to tell her." Kerri looks at me. "I told her living with Jo doesn't mean you don't need her. She's so afraid if she lets you go, she'll never get you back. I hope I'm not putting words in your mouth, but I told her choosing Jo over her didn't mean she was losing you forever."

No, Mom. I still need you. I always will.

Kerri goes, "Don't make a liar out of me."

"What?" I'd never —

She cracks a smile.

There are laugh lines around her eyes. She has teasing eyes. Cool eyes.

"Don't get me wrong," Kerri says. "I didn't do anything. She's the one who decided. She called Jo. That was hard."

When I don't say anything, she adds, "She's going to miss you, Nick. So much. You don't even know. I'll miss you too."

"Yeah, right."

"I will."

I meet Kerri's eyes. She means it.

I feel crappy for all the grief and heartache I've caused her and Mom. All the hate I laid on her, on both of them. Mom needs Kerri. She'll be alone when I go. Yeah, Mom'll miss me, but she'll be okay with Kerri here.

Mom loves Kerri. Kerri loves her. That I know for sure.

"Thanks," I say.

Kerri tilts her head. "I didn't do anything."

"Yeah, you did." She stuck up for me. Kerri risked her relationship with Mom to be on my side.

Like she's reading my thoughts, Kerri's eyes get all watery. "It was nothing."

Yeah, it was nothing. It only saved my life.

We sit for a minute. In peace. Quiet. I tell her what I should've told her a long time ago, a hundred times. "You're an awesome chef."

"Thanks. That means a lot coming from Captain Potato Chip."

I laugh. It feels good to laugh.

"I better get back," I tell her.

"Yeah," she goes. "It's dangerous to leave those two together for more than thirty seconds." She crosses her eyes and sticks out her tongue.

I grin. I push to my feet.

"Nick." She grabs my pant leg.

When I turn, she lets go. "Nothing." She shakes her head at the floor.

"No," I tell her. "It wasn't nothing. It was everything."

Mom and Jo

Mom and Jo are sitting together on the bed with my scrapbook open between them. "What do you think this is?" Mom asks Jo.

"For crying out loud," Jo says. "He kept those?"

They both glance up at me in the doorway. "Kept what?" I wander over. They're the stitches from my chin. The Scotch tape gluing them on the page is yellowed and peeling. I'll need to replace it soon. "You remember," I say. "When I was three?" I'd just turned three.

Mom shakes her head. "I can't believe the doctor let you keep the stitches."

"He didn't," Jo says. "I had to fish them out of the trash."

"What?" Mom curls a lip.

"Don't you remember? We went in to have them removed, and Nick was screaming bloody murder and we couldn't shut him up. He kept blubbering about how he had to have those stitches, he wanted to keep those stitches forever and ever. We should've known then there was something not quite right with this kid. We should've gotten a refund from the sperm bank."

I knuckle Jo's head. She arm-wrestles me to the floor and pins me under her fist.

Mom flips a page and breathes, "Oh my God. I wondered where this went." She unfolds the picture taped to the page. "I remember this so clearly," she says. "Third grade. Mrs. Ivey. She was your favorite teacher, wasn't she, Nick?"

Is Mom serious? "Oh yeah," I say sarcastically. I meet Jo's eyes, and we about bust a gut.

Mom smirks knowingly. She traces a finger over the clouds and says, "I always loved this drawing."

Jo relinquishes her hold on me and tilts her head. "Me too." She smiles down at my picture.

Me three, I think. It's the one where I'm squished between Mom and Jo.

Mom refolds the picture gently and turns the page. "A watermelon seed?"

My throat catches. Please, I pray, don't make me explain.

"Well" — Mom closes the book and stands — "you'll want to take this with you." She hands me the book.

We're all done packing my room. I rise to my feet and hold the scrapbook across my arms for a moment, then extend it to Mom. "Why don't you keep it? Put it in a safe place for now. I'll probably start a new one anyway." My birthday is coming up. With my birthday money, I think I'll buy an album. A bigger one.

"Yeah," Jo pipes up, "Part Two. Nicholas Nathaniel Thomas Tyler. Retard, Thief, Pervert, and Pack Rat. Coming soon on DVD."

I sneer at Jo, and she grabs my ankle. She flips me over onto the bed. Before I can react, she's on me, tickling me, digging into my ribs. I'm giggling and fighting her off.

I look over at Mom. She's not smiling. "She started it," I say, pushing Jo off. I rearrange my twisted clothes.

Mom reaches into her pocket and retrieves an object. She hands it to me. "Don't forget this," she says.

It's my cell.

I take it and flip it open. "Are all my numbers still stored? Yours and Kerri's?"

Mom nods and smiles. "I put the address of the new house in your memos too. So you won't forget."

"I won't forget. I'll call you," I add. "I'll call you tonight."

Jo hits me with an overstuffed garbage bag. "Grab your poncho and sleeping bag on the way out, Saint Nick. Since I only have the one futon, you'll be camping in the carport."

"You think," I mutter.

"I know." She hitches her chin for me to scram.

I sling the garbage bag over my shoulder and pretend to leave. I get as far as the hallway. Jo says, "Erin —"

I lower the bag quietly and flatten myself against the wall to listen.

"I'll send you child support," Mom says. "I'll look into the legalities of everything. You may have to officially adopt him to gain custody or legal guardianship. I'm not sure what's involved, but don't worry about it."

Jo says, "I'm not. Like I said, we'll work it out. That's not what I wanted to say. I wanted to . . ." She stalls. Her voice falters. "I want to thank you. For trusting me."

Mom doesn't answer. I wonder if she'll tell her the truth.

Jo adds, "I love you for this. More than you'll ever know."

"You'll never forgive me, though. Will you?"

Jo sighs. "I forgive you, Erin. I just want us all to be happy. Life's too short, you know? We have to make each day count. Isn't that the Erin Tyler, cancer survivor, philosophy of life? If it's not, it should be."

Mom doesn't reply. I sense tension in the air. That staggering silence. Mom says softly, "Thank you, Jo. I love you too. I know you don't believe that. . . ."

"I do," Jo says quickly. "Let's just get past it, okay? Is there a law that says we can't be friends?"

I envision Mom consulting The Book, the one in her head. Reading off The Rules. "Take care of him," she says. "Take care of each other."

I smile inside. I think she finally gets it. I can't see through the wall, but I know what's happening. They're hugging. This powerful force rises up around them, between them, and I know what it is. Who it is.

I squeeze my eyes and vow to never forget this day, this second, this defining moment of my life.

When I open my eyes, Mom's beside me. Jo's behind me. Kerri's there too. I think, Wow. How lucky can I be?

Then I think, Lucky? I have three moms. I have to start planning now for Mother's Day.